Action This Day: Aspects of History Short Story Collection

Table of Contents

Introduction

Action This Day is a collection of short stories set during the Second World War, by bestselling authors of the genre. These tales, which serve as a taster menu for various successful series, encompass murder, espionage, courage, humour and history. You'll find plenty to enjoy, from the build-up to war in the US, the war on the Home Front, the invasion of Germany and war in the air and on sea.

As well as curating a series of entertaining and engaging stories, we were keen to interview each author about their inspiration, their fascination with WW2 and how they put their novels together. One of the purposes of the collection is to help introduce audiences to new series.

If you have a keen interest in the Second World War then do visit our substack (aspectsofhistory.substack.com), where you'll find we've just launched with contributions from Saul David and Roger Moorhouse, and much much more to come. You can also follow us at @aspectshistory on Twitter.

Finally, if these stories inspire you to write your own historical fiction, or if you've already written a history book or historical novel, please do get in touch with me through our website. Aspects of History is always looking to help publish and promote new and established authors. If you have the right story, we can help you tell it.

Oliver Webb-Carter
Editor & Co-Founder, Aspects of History

Warriors Return, by Timothy Ashby

I saw my father last night.

I was staying at my family home, tidying up loose ends, reluctantly sorting and discarding centuries of family relics prior to putting the old house on the market. Mother had died a month earlier in a nursing home at the age of ninety-eight. I strove to sense her lingering presence, but she had decisively passed on into whatever purgatory awaits those lost in senile dementia. Melancholy seemed to permeate every damp, dusty room and piece of mildewed furniture. As I half-heartedly shifted stacks of papers, my mood darkened, reflective of the atmosphere. The house itself seems to be accusing me of disrupting and destroying the once happy abode of people who had lived here and cherished it.

Yet, I had no choice. My task was heart-breaking but necessary. I would be eighty years old next year, an old man yet still in reasonable health. Mother's care had taken all her meagre savings and some of my own. The house must be sold to pay the debts. And I, a widower, could not have lived in such a large place even if I had the means to do so.

Eventually, I gave up and made myself comfortable in a frayed armchair with a glass of Balvenie to hand. I raised the glass in a toast to my ancestors, asking their forgiveness. Cocooned amid familiar books and musty furnishings in the library, surrounded by silver frames displaying fading ancestors, I felt strangely at peace. Tilly, my ancient Jack Russell, dozed at my feet.

Warmed by the fire, momentarily free from the burden of generations, my eyelids closed.

Tilly's whine, a mournful little cry of confusion, awoke me. A chill permeated the room despite the fire. Then I saw him.

He leaned over the old library table with his back towards me, shoulders broad under the Royal Air Force tunic. He turned, allowing me a glimpse of his profile. Tilly whimpered, backing under my chair. Although his features were shadowed, I knew every detail of my father's 24-year-old face.

He looked at me, expression pleading. The cold deepened. I longed to go to him but felt paralysed. He turned back to the desk and pointed his index finger. Then he sighed – a faint, weary sound on the border between imagination and reality.

Tilly barked, shattering the atmosphere. My father was gone.

His visit was nothing new. I had seen him numerous times from the earliest days of my childhood, before I knew who he had been and what he had become.

He was lost in May 1944, less than six weeks before my birth. His Spitfire disappeared on a mission over Normandy, place and circumstances unknown. Vanished, he became just another name on a long roster of Kentish warriors missing in action since the days of Agincourt. Resting place unknown, father's existence was reduced to a brass plaque on the wall of our parish church, near memorials to uncles lost in the Great War and an ancestor who perished in the Crimea.

Mother never remarried. Her temporary stay with father's parents became permanent. As the years passed my grandparents joined their predecessors in the churchyard, leaving an empty plot beside them in the hope that their only son would one day come home.

I first saw the handsome man in the uniform on my fourth Christmas Eve. Nanny had gone away for the holidays, and I was left on my own upstairs. Exploring, I found a bedroom door ajar. Creeping inside, I discovered an Aladdin's cave of delights for a small boy: toy soldiers, model airplanes, cricket bats. While I was playing with a tin car, I noticed a man standing in the corner. He had sad blue eyes that matched his uniform. I said hello but he did not reply, so I returned to my play. He was gone when I looked again.

I found out later that the room had been my father's. My grandparents never changed anything in it, and neither did my mother. I saw the man several times there when I went in to play. I knew he liked me, even though he never spoke.

A year later I came across my mother weeping in her bedroom, head bowed over a photograph. I hugged her and asked who the man in the picture was.

"Your daddy. But he went away before you were born and is never coming back."

I was happy to know that the nice man in the blue uniform was my father, but confused about him never coming back. I cheerfully explained to her that he was a regular visitor.

Mother questioned me at length, first incredulous and then accepting my innocent account as I described her husband in detail. She shut herself away for several days after that. When she emerged, she seemed happier, as if she believed that my father had returned to watch over us.

When I went away to school, I came across a quote by some Asian philosopher that embedded itself in my mind: "The line between life and death is not thicker than an eyelid." My visits home became rarer, and a year could go by before I saw my father's ghost. And sometimes he was just a shade, a flicker in the darkness at the top of the staircase or the barest glimpse of a blue-coated figure at the corner of my vision. Once I asked Mother if she had seen him, but she shushed me and changed the subject. So, I will never know if I was his only connection to the earthly life.

Or perhaps he was drawn to the house where he had grown up and which would soon be divested of father's material connections.

As I aged, I began to question whether I had actually experienced visitation from a long-lost pilot. Was I delusional? I read about the paranormal, and had several pleasant meetings with mother's vicar where the sherry flowed freely and he preferred to sermonise about the Holy Ghost rather than the one who I thought haunted our family home. My grandparents could not bring themselves to talk about their son. Their profound sorrow lasted until the day that each died.

I sought psychological counselling, and was told by the therapist that ghosts didn't exist and from childhood, I was mourning the father I never knew and inventing his presence. Many children

4

have imaginary playmates, the eminent psychologist told me condescendingly. *You* had an imaginary *father*. Nothing, neither books nor therapy, served to comfort me. I was unconvinced that I was delusional, sure of my own observations. For decades I had the niggling feeling that my father was appearing for a reason that I was unable to understand.

After seeing the blue-uniformed figure again, I lay awake all night, not from supernatural fear but pondering the great mystery of the young man I had undoubtedly seen in the library, replaying every moment of something that had lasted mere seconds. At a few minutes past 3:00 in the morning, I realized that father was seeking my help, and had been doing so for years.

At daylight, I returned to where he had stood in the library. A few old Baedeker maps were strewn across the desk. Next to them was a photo of my mother as a teenage girl, smiling winsomely at the photographer. She had once told me that my father had taken the picture on their brief honeymoon to Windermere in 1942.

I stood where I had seen him and tried to duplicate the way in which he had pointed. Normandy lay beneath my hand on a large-scale map of northern France. With mounting excitement, I grabbed a magnifying glass and scanned the map. At first, nothing unusual caught my eye. Then I saw it.

To the casual observer, it would have appeared as a water stain, a teardrop perhaps. But under the magnifier, I noticed the mark's resemblance to an RAF eagle emblem. It lay near a village called Montbrieu.

I caught a late-night ferry to Calais and drove through the early morning, stopping only for coffee and petrol near Rouen. Passing through Montbrieu, I headed south with the map on my knees, not trusting the newfangled GPS on my mobile phone. After two miles I began to despair, seeing nothing but open fields. I stopped and reversed into a lane to turn around. In the rearview mirror I saw a distant figure in a blue uniform. When I turned to look it had vanished.

I climbed a fence and slogged through a muddy field towards the spot where I had seen the figure. A recently excavated drainage ditch bisected the field, and I walked along it until I noticed a large piece of corroded sheet metal. Sliding down the bank into knee-deep water, I brushed soil from a crumpled fuselage section until a faded RAF roundel was exposed.

I found a room in a nearby Bed and Breakfast, sought out the local gendarmes, and made a series of calls to London and Gloucester after searching on Google. Then I waited, returning to the crash site each day to maintain vigil against scavengers.

The MOD's Joint Casualty and Compassionate Centre (JCCC) - the 'MOD War Detectives' - was very efficient. They had a team on the site a week later. Assisted by gendarmes, they excavated down to the aircraft's cockpit. I turned away as they removed the shattered canopy. Shortly afterwards one of the excavators came over and handed me something.

"Found this on the pilot," he said. "Remarkably well-preserved, isn't it?"

It was a leather wallet. I opened it with shaking fingers. Atop RAF identity papers was a photo of a young woman identical to the one I had seen on the library table in my family home.

Interview

Can you first please tell us a little more about the series and/or character that your short story is based around?

The ghost of a missing RAF pilot who has haunted his son since the boy's birth. The spectre is trying to convey a message to the son. The series itself is set around FBI Special Agent Seth Armitage, a US Marines veteran haunted by the carnage of the Western Front, back to the Bureau to investigate the mystery. J. Edgar Hoover recruits him to investigate various mysteries that take him from the United States to Nazi Germany during the 1920s and 30s.

What first attracted you to the period you write about? How do you approach researching your novels?

I look for unusual historical events – genuine mysteries that you find in both my novels *Devil's Den* and *In Shadowland*. I feature events and figures I'm fascinated by, such as the jazz era and Teddy Roosevelt.

If there was one moment in history you could witness, featured in one of your novels, what would it be?

It's tough to limit it to one! It would have to be the Battle of New Orleans when Andrew Jackson saw off the British in the War of 1812. We remember it well over here in the States, for the Brits, less so. If you were to ask me about WWII, I'd say the attack on Pearl Harbor. Truly 'a date that will live in infamy.'

What do you think makes so many readers attracted to reading about the Second World War?

WW2 is still within living memory, and there is a vast amount of material available including testimony by men and women who lived through the era. We've seen moving pictures, and increasingly colour images. The war dominated the 20th century, and it was also a war that was simple: good against evil. The Allies

7

really did defeat an terrible ideology, not just once, but again during the Cold War.

Which other authors, fiction or non-fiction, do you admire who write about the Second World War?

I'm very much a fan of Saul David's *Crucible of Hell* and *Devil Dogs*, both dealing with the Pacific theatre. I also admire Rick Atkinson, in particular *The Guns at Last Light* the third of his Liberation trilogy.

If you could invite three figures from WW2 to dinner, who would they be and why?

Churchill, Guderian and Theodore Roosevelt Jr. would make for an entertaining dinner, although I doubt Guderian and Winston would be on speaking terms. Teddy and Winston would get on probably.

What piece of advice would you give to other historical novelists out there, who are just starting out?

Be exacting in getting even the most minor historical details correct – it matters, your readers will tell you if you don't! But also, make sure the plot moves along, so don't get too bogged down with the history.

Can you tell us a little more about your next project?

My next project will be a large-scale supernatural thriller, with a WWII connection – but I can't reveal too much more just yet!

Lies, Damned Lies and Misinformation,
by Alan Bardos

July 1938

Polite applause crept around Wilhelmshaven's ancient lecture hall; to Danny Nichols it was like thunder. He grasped the lectern and stared at the fresh-faced members of the Christian Students for Peace symposium, neatly sat in ascending rows that dwarfed him.

The crowd began to murmur, sensing his apprehension. Nichols thought of what his father had told him before he was made to address his congregation, "Come on old man, you're rather letting the side down." Reverend Nichols would wake most nights screaming, reliving the Somme and Passchendaele. It had terrified Danny as a child and made him resolutely believe in pacifism.

Nichols knew exactly what to say of course. He'd spoken at these types of events from Oxford to Prague, but it never paid to be too eager. He worried that he would end up like all those other people who shouted their beliefs at the tops of their voices and didn't realise what utter nonsense they were talking.

'When Herr Hitler came to power in Germany, it seemed to me perfectly reasonable that he would want to redress the harsh terms of the Treaty of Versailles. I therefore wholeheartedly supported my government's policy of appeasing this aspiration.'

Nichols didn't recognise his voice: it had taken on a nasal twang, but his German was flawless.

'I knew the only way to reach an understanding and breakdown the barriers that were threatening Europe was to start a dialogue. To that end, I learnt German and applied to study at Vienna University, so I could better tour Europe in the name of peace and meet other young people united in the cause of appeasement.'

Nichols paused, to allow more polite clapping. He didn't see the need to mention that he specifically went to Vienna to study under Fraud, and the German intervention in Austria had now made that impossible. Nichols could still hear the drone of German aircraft flying over Vienna the day Hitler marched in. It was the threat from the sky that really scared him.

'It all seems pretty simple to me. The Treaty of Versailles was made by statesmen stuck in the Nineteenth Century, who made a Nineteenth Century peace to settle a Twentieth Century War - dividing up the spoils and imposing guilt and reparations. It is up to us to make sure our statesmen learn the lessons of the past and find a better peace, a Twentieth Century peace. Especially now modern bombers can lay waste to whole cities, as happened in Guernica less than a year ago.'

That raised a murmur of concern from the delegates. Nichols focused on the fine stonework of the auditorium. Each block was intricately designed to support the next tier, in a solid mass that held up the roof. Nichols had tried to construct his mind in such a fashion of strength and self-assurance.

'Of course, I cannot speak to the rights and wrongs of German foreign policy: that is politics. Nonetheless I commend Herr Hitler for abandoning his plans to occupy Czechoslovakia in May and I hope he will continue to settle his territorial claims peacefully. And, like me, will make friends across Europe in the hope of creating a cultural understanding. I just have one last thing to say to you all – Prost!'

There was a muted response of 'Prost'. Nichols was not a man to arouse great passion, even amongst students for drinking.

No one joined him after the conference. Nichols sipped Riesling, enjoying the sweet wine and the embarrassed looks as the delegates clamoured to avoid him. He couldn't blame them. A banner with a finely stitched dove and Swastika looked down on them and neatly summed up the event. Everyone supported the idea of peace, but he supposed for a German to be too enthusiastic might bring them to the attention of the authorities.

A few embarrassed glances from the crowd told him he should leave, so they could have some fun. Nichols glanced at his watch; it was time he got some air.

The seafront was filled with rowdy sailors from the *Kriegsmarine* in blue and gold uniforms. Nichols moved out of their way and stopped to look out at the harbour. Wilhelmshaven might be one of the less fashionable resorts, but it was the German's only deep-water port and was full of ships.

He had always been fascinated by things that float; taking his boat out on adventures that would be considered far too dangerous by his parents, so developing the ability to lie had been vital. Deceit and deception to get what he wanted had always come naturally to him. Nichols wondered if lying to a vicar was a really very wicked sin, when as a result he got to go sailing.

'Quite a beautiful sight, isn't she?'

Nichols realised he'd been paying too much attention to a large battleship under construction across the bay. She was indeed beautiful, in a threatening and sinister kind of way.

He glanced around thinking he was being addressed by an SS man and was relieved to see a portly boy of eighteen in an ill-fitting black suit. The sort of boy instantly picked on, but the most heroic person Nichols had met.

'Beautiful isn't quite the word I'd use Willi.' Nichols patted him on the shoulder and walked on. He was more jumpy than he'd realised.

'The *Tirpitz's* hull will soon be completed,' the boy said falling into step with him. Nichols couldn't help but think of Willi as a boy even though he was only two years younger than himself. Nichols supposed it was his boyish enthusiasm.

'*Tirpitz is* the sister ship of the *Bismarck*, the most powerful battleship afloat. Imagine Germany's naval power when she is fully completed.'

The thought of the two of them rippling through the North Sea towards his homeland terrified Nichols. He wondered how, and more accurately who, would stop them. Since the events at Guernica, Nichols had found himself taking more of an interest in air power and the growing belief that it would soon surpass the mighty battleship. In America, an Air Force General named Mitchell had sunk a battleship through aerial bombardment. Although that had been under test conditions, looking at the size of the *Tirpitz* now, Nichols found it hard to believe that would ever happen if the ship was shooting back.

11

'I suppose she wouldn't have much trouble getting to England, would she Willi?'

'Oh no, none at all, her range is far greater than fifteen thousand kilometres.'

Nichols sat on a bench and looked around. There was no one within earshot and he smiled for Willi to continue. Nichols took careful note as Willi reeled off a list of facts about the *Tirpitz's* armament and armour with sickening precision. It seemed incredible that any ship could be so powerful. Nichols was awed that this plucky boy would risk everything to give him the information.

He had met Willi at a student conference in Danzig. As a Quaker, Willi was horrified to have been made to work at Wilhelmshaven Naval shipyard. Like Nichols, he felt that sharing information about the capacity of weapons was the only way to avoid catastrophe. Nichols had made many such acquaintances across Europe, attending peace rallies and writing articles.

Nichols had an interminable journey back to Vienna; the train was shunted backwards and forwards, delayed by high priority traffic. At every jolt he waited for the shrill call of police whistles and the baying of dogs, before leather coated men stormed his carriage.

The return to Vienna gave little relief to the constant need to be on guard. He still hadn't got used to the change in mood that had permeated his favourite city.

Nichols had spent a blissful year studying and enjoying everything Viennese cafe society had to offer, and then in March Hitler had proclaimed the Anschluss.

Nichols had watched helplessly as Hitler paraded triumphantly through Vienna with all his military might. After that, philosophy and psychology did not seem important, and reasoned debate was futile when confronted with the hate of the baying mobs that forced the city's Jews to scrub the streets.

The barbarity of it appalled Nichols and the fact that he was unable to stop it made him sick. He had never felt so powerless or humiliated. All he could think to do was to go to the British Embassy and register his protest.

He'd met Kendrick, the head of British intelligence in Vienna, outside the passport office scaring off brown shirts who were harassing Jews trying to get British papers. Nichols didn't think he'd met a finer man and gladly allowed himself to be recruited. His peace campaigning made the perfect cover to collect intelligence. Nichols reasoned that he could use information to stop Hitler, rather than bullets. It was, he felt, still a pacifist stance, but a more robust and assertive one.

A few days later he was introduced to his handler Johnny Swift, a hedonist of the worst type who was rumoured to be one of Churchill's backbench drinking pals. He delighted in shocking Nichols, insisting they meet in his favourite watering hole, a cabaret club of the more vulgar variety.

Nichols found Swift in a corner booth surrounded by cartoon burlesque baroque figures on the walls. He was drinking champagne and watching a pair of twins perform some kind of striptease, accompanied by gypsy violinists playing one of Brahms' Hungarian dances.

They sat and watched the performance for a while, then Swift acknowledged him by turning his champagne bottle over in its bucket and signalling for another.

'I trust you have something of interest to have interrupted my afternoon repast?' Swift said and smiled dryly. Nichols imagined in his day Swift might have been quite a player. Now in his forties, a career spent on the frontline of the world's fleshpots was catching up with him; hard lines were drawn across his face like a treasure map to the best brothel in town.

'As a matter of fact, I do.' Nichols handed Swift a note of the information he'd got from Willi. Swift looked pleased. He told him that London was desperate to get their hands on anything about the *Tirpitz*.

'Excellent. This agent of yours is shaping up into a little gold mine.'

Nichols felt a little uncomfortable with the idea that he was running an agent, but Willi was certainly a gold mine. He'd already provided information on German U-boats that could prove invaluable in warning London of German capabilities and highlighting the need to avert war.

'It all seems a little too good to be true though doesn't it?' Swift asked and tilted his head in the questioning way a parent might employ with a confused child.

'I have spent the past year studying psychology under the finest mind in the field, so I think I might know when I'm being deceived. If that's what you mean.'

Swift laughed and Nichols hoped he hadn't sounded pompous, but he'd never been more sure of anything in his life.

'I wonder if you'll feel the same way when you've finished your degree.' Swift took a drink and allowed himself a glance at the stage before returning to his work.

'You're my best operative Danny, so I'll trust your judgement on this matter. You have a stupid face, well-defined no doubt, but totally lacking in guile. A face that women trust, and men tell their secrets, a face people would think incapable of deceit.'

'I see,' Nichols expected that was what was meant by a backhanded compliment.

'Oh come, Danny Boy. All I meant was it's perfectly possible that this Willi character is what you say he is and trusts you enough to betray his country for you - in the name of peace.'

Nichols wasn't sure that made him feel any better.

'I'm due to meet Willi again in Czechoslovakia next month for a prayer and reflection seminar.' Nichols said pointedly to show he hadn't lost all his values.

Swift stifled a laugh, 'If there is a Czechoslovakia next month.'

'But Hitler has been put in his place. Mr Chamberlin made it perfectly clear -'

'He did no such thing, The Germans simply weren't ready to invade and Czechoslovakia is well protected. Hitler won't be able to waltz into Prague as he did here. Not unless we let him at the next conference.'

Nichols was horrified after all his efforts, 'But surely if we allow him the Sudetenland ...'

ACTION THIS DAY

'Do you think he'd stop there? I doubt it. The Sudetenland was not part of Germany before the war – nor was Austria for that matter. So you can hardly use your snivelling little argument about righting the wrongs of Versailles. My God, do you think the Germans would have shown us any mercy if the boot had been on the other foot? Look at the peace they imposed on the Russians at Brest-Litovsk, half their country was taken!'

Nichols found Swift a little coarse after his bouts of afternoon drinking, but there was some logic to what he had to say.

'There was an increase in rail traffic towards the Czech border. It totally disrupted my return journey.'

'Yes, there are many such reports, but they could just be manoeuvres. Our job is to find out what the Bosche's intentions are towards the Czech border. I have a line on a source in the German Staff, who can tell us precisely that. For a price.'

'You want me to go back to Germany?' Nichols asked anxiously.

'No, Prague. My contact got the information from Czech intelligence.'

'That's slightly better, I suppose.'

'That's the spirit. Reminds me of myself at your age. Just tread lightly. The Germans are starting to round up our agents.'

Nichols always marvelled at the fairy-tale atmosphere of Prague's old town square that became more sinister as he turned into a Kafkaesque warren of vaulted arcades. A flicker of shadow in the twilight caught Nichols' eye and he ducked behind a pillar. The shadow became a drunk staggering home on the cobbles. Nichols felt himself breathe and quickly scuffled down the steps of a crowded cellar bar. He stood at the darkly varnished bar and ordered a pils. Nichols had not really been one for drink before he met Swift, he reflected and took a gulp.

A man with a scar on his face limped towards him. Nichols tried not to clench his hands around his glass too tightly. The man passed him, and Nichols saw a glint of light on his pince-nez. Nichols finished his beer and felt that the money he had in his pocket was gone, and that there was a wad of paper there.

15

Nichols continued to be gripped by the same repressive feeling of impending doom on the train back to Vienna. He spent the journey summarising the typed documents he'd received and burnt the originals in the lavatory. There had been something unnerving in Swift's warning and it almost felt inevitable when a group of men in fedoras and leather trench coats grabbed him outside the station.

Nichols was left in a brightly lit cell. Unable to sleep or see daylight, he lost track of time. His only connection to the outside world was the sound of screaming echoing up the corridor, but even that could have been his mind playing tricks.

After what felt like a week, Nichols was strapped into a chair with a desk light shoved in his face. He could hear footsteps behind the light.

'What the hell is going on?' Lack of sleep had left Nichols in something of a blue funk.

'Really you have no idea why you've been brought here?' An amused voice asked.

'Someone must have been telling lies about Danny Nichols.' Nichols said. He heard a chuckle.

'I think not. Someone has been playing games with Danny Nichols.' A grim face briefly came into focus behind the light.

'You may address me as Detective Inspector Sauer and if you answer my questions, we shall all get along famously.'

Nichols heard a second person chuckling, in the corner behind him.

'You have no right to do this. I'm a British citizen, a student working for peace.' Nichols felt himself unravelling, his self-control crashing down and it was that which he found terrifying.

'May I ask what you care about Czechoslovakia – a sham country, cobbled together from the remnants of the Austro-Hungarian monarchy?'

'People have a right to self-determination.'

'Yes, but it only seems to be some of the people. There were no prayer meetings when the victors were taking chunks of Hungary

16

and Austria, displacing thousands of its people and stealing their homes.'

'I'm sorry if that happened to you, I'm working to try and redress injustice.'

Nichols heard a loud snort. His interrogator did not want his sympathy and thought his efforts worthless. Nichols felt his face flush, his anger helping to pull himself together.

'I wouldn't expect someone like you to understand the nobility of peace, putting the greater good first.'

'Since when is committing acts of espionage in a foreign state working for peace?'

'I beg your pardon -'

'Don't waste my time. I know you've been collecting information about the Reich. Tell me who sent you to Prague.'

'My father the Reverend Gerald Nichols enrolled me into the International Christian Appeasement Movement.' Nichols tried to picture the solid structure of his church.

Sauer kicked the chair, 'Who is your contact in the Vienna Passport office?'

Nichols felt himself jolt, not sure how they knew about that. Somewhere in the shadows he heard the menacing creak of floorboards; there was definitely someone else in the room. He fought to maintain an impassive face. He knew he must stick to his story. If he admitted to anything he was finished.

'I can't imagine anyone in the British passport office would be engaged in anything like that.'

'If that is the case, who have you been passing your intelligence to?'

'I don't know anything about intelligence.'

'Don't play these childish games. You were carrying a large amount of statistical material about German troop dispositions.'

Nichols' sleep-deprived mind swirled, and he began to panic. They'd caught him out in a childish lie and in a moment of clarity he realised what he must say. He just hoped Swift had been right about people thinking his face incapable of deceit.

'Forgive me Detective Inspector Sauer, you are perfectly correct. I have been mistaken.'

'Of course.'

'There is a misunderstanding. I have not been conducting espionage, but I have been gathering information.'

'Don't trifle with me.'

'I'm sorry I didn't understand your questions, but none of it is secret. I've been working for the peace movement, trying to foster peace through shared knowledge. If mutually assured destruction is inevitable, then why would either side go to war?'

'Your childish motives are of no consequence. The fact that you admit you have been working for British Intelligence is all that matters.'

'I'm completely unaware of any connection to British Intelligence. I write for a pacifist international periodical, but the British may have seen my articles along with statesmen in Germany, France, and Russia.'

Sauer laughed, 'You really believe that nonsense! Very well I see no point in continuing this. You are clearly what you say you are. Your parents have also made quite a fuss. They're threatening to write a letter to the Times.'

'What?'

'It is now necessary to release you to prevent any distractions from the coming peace conference in Munich.' Sauer turned the light off and Nichols saw a stern face that seemed to reinforce the belief that he was just a naive boy.

'You know, of course, that your so-called peace movement is riddled with spies.'

'I think I'd know if it was, I am a student of the human mind,' Nichols said unable to contain his feeling of triumph. He heard a hissing giggle and a familiar face appeared from the shadows.

'Willi, they got you too...' then Nichols realised his mistake. 'You're one of them!'

'I've been playing you for a fool - a bloody fool!' Willi's glee was nearly enough to crack Nichols' reserve.

'A useful fool, nonetheless, we've been using you to plant false information. To make our enemies think we are stronger than we really are, and that destruction would be inevitable if they stood in our way - their destruction not ours.'

18

Nichols remained silent. They were only telling him this because no one would listen to him now. The legend of Germany's overwhelming strength had been firmly planted in the minds of Western politicians.

Swift organised a car to get them out of Vienna the following day and was in a buoyant mood when he collected Nichols from his rooms.

'You did a splendid job.'

'But the Germans nabbed me.'

'I shouldn't worry. The whole network's being rolled up. The Germans are clearing the board before they swallow up Czechoslovakia.'

'Then there will be a war?'

'Eventually.'

'I lost the information that could have stopped it.'

'Misinformation actually.'

'I'm sorry?'

'I played a little prank on the Germans. That chap in Prague who prepared the documents is an old friend of mine – a former Austro-Hungarian officer.'

'You set me up…'

'Look it seemed pretty obvious to me that we were losing the intelligence war. The Germans had penetrated our networks and were misleading and misdirecting us. The information you were getting seemed grossly exaggerated and contradicted our other sources.'

'So I was sacrificed to plant false information?'

'It wasn't exactly false. Just exaggerated, to make the Germans think we knew more than we did and to try and slow them down as they looked for a phantom spy running a network in Prague and reordered their troop dispositions. "Lies, damned lies and statistics", as Churchill says.'

'I believe it was Disraeli actually.'

Nichols gazed out of the window as the city he loved flashed by. He was exhausted and totally defeated, played by both sides.

'You have a feel for this type of work Danny.'

'Being made to look a fool.' The shame of being so totally taken in was overwhelming.

'For lying and deception, even to yourself. You fooled the Gestapo into thinking you weren't working for SIS and more importantly you kept your mouth shut about me.'

Nichols didn't see it that way. He was just trying to be whatever the person he was speaking to wanted. Something he'd learnt watching his father talk to his parishioners; people he criticized in private to his wife were praised in public to the congregation. The Reverend was a man for all seasons if ever there was one.

'Just learn from your mistakes Danny boy. Now you've been knocked off your high horse you'll be more wary next time.'

'Next time?' Nichols felt a shudder run through him. The only thing his sleep-starved mind knew was that, after what he'd just been through, he had no wish to be a spy.

'I'm going to need people like you Nichols - your country is going to need people like you.'

'No thank you Mr Swift. From what I've seen the best way to protect my country is either to join the navy, or the air force. I expect air power will be the decisive factor in any coming war.'

'Very well, if that's your final word, I'm not going to force you. I know what that's like. I have contacts in the Admiralty who can organise a Board for the Fleet Air Arm.'

The rocking motion of the car finally put Nichols to sleep, as he watched the Vienna suburbs drift away. He'd left behind the dark world he was so clearly ill-equipped for.

Interview

Can you first please tell us a little more about the series and/or character that your short story is based around?

The short story is a prequel to the novel I'm currently working on, which is the first in a new World War II series that follows Danny Nichols as he moves from the Fleet Air Arm to Intelligence and Special Operations. The short story introduces Nichols and features Johnny Swift, the lead character from my World War I series, who passes the baton on to Nichols and as the person pulling the strings this time, has a bit of fun at Nichols' expense.

What first attracted you to the period you write about? How do you approach researching your novels?

British Intelligence is famous for deceiving the Germans during WWII in Operations like Mince Meat and Fortitude. In the period just before WWII it was a different story. German Intelligence was running rampant across Europe. They pulled off a number of coups against the British, most notoriously capturing key British Intelligence officers at Venlo in 1939. This enabled them to roll up Britain's intelligence networks in Western Europe. The Germans also fed false information to British Intelligence, which probably influenced British foreign policy at the time. I thought that would make an interesting basis for a short story and is something I'd like to explore further one day.

I'm still developing and refining my research process, but my starting point is to try and read as many books as I can on the subject I'm writing about. I whittle that down to a few key books that are my guiding lights and others which I use for specific details about an event or place, such as memoirs and first-hand accounts. When writing 'The Dardanelles Conspiracy' I supplemented this by visiting the reading room of the Imperial War Museum and the National Archive. I also try to visit as many places where the novel is set as I can, to see firsthand what it looks like and get a feel for the place.

21

If there was one moment in history you could witness, featured in one of your novels, what would it be?

I would like to witness Archduke Franz Ferdinand's visit to Sarajevo on 28th June 1914. I have spent a lot of time reading about it and imagining the events around the visit, what the atmosphere was like and what the city looked like. I would love to see how much I got right on that epoch-defining day, after all the contradictory accounts I've read. However, if I was there on that day, I wouldn't be able to stand by and watch the assassination of the Archduke and his wife Sophie and would have to try and change history.

On a more aesthetic note, it would be incredible to see Mata Hari dance in Paris during the *Belle époque.*

What do you think makes so many readers attracted to reading about the Second World War?

For me, the Second World War is a real life story of triumph over adversity and coming back from the brink to win against the odds. Most people and their families were touched by WWII, and it is therefore very much alive and in the collective consciousness. People have grown up listening to stories from grandparents and parents about their experiences, which is incredibly powerful and certainly began my interest in history. Added to this is the fact that the world we live in was shaped so dramatically by the war.

Which other authors, fiction or non-fiction, do you admire who write about the Second World War?

I should start by mentioning Helen Fry's 'Spymaster: The Man Who Saved MI6' and Christopher Andrew's 'Secret Service', as they inspired my short story and are both great books about the intelligence war. In terms of other nonfiction writers, I admire Giles Milton, Damian Lewis, Soul David, Ian Kershaw, Antony Beevor, Gordon W. Prange, and Ben Macintyre.

In terms of fiction, the writers I really admire are Herman Wouk, James Jones, Nicholas Monsarrat, Evelyn Waugh, Alan Furst and Robert Harris and Ken Follett.

ACTION THIS DAY

If you could invite three figures from WW2 to dinner, who would they be and why?
This is likely to change every time I write a new book about WWII, but at the moment the people who have inspired and informed the novel I'm working on were all spies; Richard Sorge, Dusko Popov and Takeo Yoshikawa. All three were 'bons vivants' and master storytellers, and would therefore make great dinner companions. Sorge was Stalin's spy in Tokyo who famously warned of the German invasion in 1941, but was ignored by Stalin. However, Sorge was also able to find out that the Japanese weren't planning to invade the USSR so Stalin could transfer troops from Siberia to push the Germans back from the gates of Moscow, one of the biggest turning points of the war. Popov is famous for his deception role before D-day in Operation Fortitude, but he also tried to warn the Americans about the Japanese attack on Pearl Harbour, and was not believed by Hoover, the head of the FBI. Yoshikawa was a Japanese spy in Hawaii who scouted out the American bases, mapping the targets for the strike force that attacked Pearl Harbour. Legend has it that it was because of his reports that the attack was planned to take place on a Sunday morning, when the fleet was in harbour and a large number of servicemen were enjoying the weekend.

What piece of advice would you give to other historical novelists out there, who are just starting out?
The secret is just to write. Get into the habit and do it every day.

Can you tell us a little more about your next project?
My next project is about Pearl Harbour and with the same character as in the short story: Danny Nichols. At the end of the short story Nichols turns his back on the Intelligence world to join the Navy. The novel takes up Nichols story as he is wounded in the Fleet Air Arm's raid on the Italian fleet in Taranto and joins Naval Intelligence. He then follows in Dusko Popov's real-life footsteps gaining the confidence of German intelligence and discovers that the Japanese plan to attack Pearl Harbour. Nichols

travels to America to warn the FBI, but the audacity of the plan is breathtaking and he is not believed.

Nichols then takes matters into his own hands.

Let Sleeping Dogs Lie, by Mark Ellis

February 1940

Detective Chief Inspector Frank Merlin stared into the mirror behind his desk and saw deep hollows under his eyes. It had been a bad week for sleep, with the Luftwaffe pounding London every night, but the evening he'd just passed in his office chair had been the worst.

Merlin had been working late at the Yard, immersed in one of his case files, when the sirens went off. He'd had three options. Try and get home in the middle of the raid, go to the Westminster shelter, or bunk up in the office. The first option was too risky. The second unappealing. The mass of sweaty frightened people, the bawling babies, the smells – no thank you. So, the office it was.

The all clear had sounded just after six thirty that morning. After perfunctory ablutions in the Assistant Commissioner's bathroom one floor up from his office, Merlin decided he had to get home and grab a couple of hours of sleep if he could.

A bus soon arrived at the Parliament Square stop and Merlin hopped on. It was pretty full. The passengers, mostly male, were a mixed bag. Some bowler-hatted City gent types. A number of labourers and workmen in rougher clothes underneath their donkey jackets. ARP wardens and civil defence workers, and a couple of fellows with black bow ties poking out of the tops of their coats – a late night on the town, he presumed.

By the time they were past Buckingham Palace, it was light enough to see what local damage the Luftwaffe had caused overnight. On Victoria Street a couple of buildings had taken hits. Fire engines were parked outside with hoses trained on the smouldering ruins. Merlin tried to remember what businesses had operated there. One was an office building, he remembered, and the other a draper's shop with flats above. He sighed. Not everyone in the flats would have gone to the shelter. More civilian deaths to add to the ever-growing German tally.

25

As the bus pulled up at a stop, he heard shouting and saw wardens racing off down the street in pursuit of someone. Looters. Looting was a big problem. He knew there'd been over 4,000 looting cases up at the Old Bailey before Christmas. There were plenty still at it. All sorts too. Wardens, home defence workers and firemen, as well as supposedly respectable civilians. Even police officers.

The bus had become less crowded, and Merlin could examine those remaining more carefully. He had a bench seat near the exit and the two men with dicky bows had moved onto the bench opposite. Both had now opened their coats and Merlin could see, as he'd guessed, that they were wearing full evening dress. They didn't speak to each other but he presumed they were together. One of the men noticed Merlin's attention and smiled pleasantly. The other, whose face was partially covered by a scarf, had started dozing.

At the Sloane Square Tube stop, the dozing man was nudged by his companion and got up. As he did so, the scarf fell away and for the first time Merlin got a good look at his face. It was long, heavily lined, with small dark eyes, and a prominent nose. The face had clearly done some living. It was also a face Merlin had seen before, the last time in the dock of the Old Bailey, when Judge Dryden had carefully placed the black cap on his bewigged head and condemned the man, Pavel Brodsky, to death.

Merlin had been eager to discuss his surprise sighting with Sergeant Bridges when he returned to the Yard later that morning, but was told the Sergeant was in Mayfair following up a lead on a recent robbery. He picked up the case file he'd been reading the previous night, a tedious City fraud the Assistant Commissioner had landed him with, and got his head down. An hour later, Constable Cole popped his head around the door and asked Merlin if he'd like a sandwich from the café round the corner.

"No thanks, Constable. I'm not hungry. I think I'll go for a lunchtime walk, though."

"Bit parky out, sir."

"So it is, but perhaps a little crisp fresh air will arouse my appetite. If anyone comes looking for me, say I'll be back in an hour or so."

Merlin headed for St James's Park where he found an empty bench overlooking the half-frozen lake. His mind turned straightaway to Pavel Brodsky. A middle-aged Czech emigré musician, Brodsky had been found guilty of murdering a woman one evening on a river towpath in Mortlake. It had been at the height of summer and still daylight. The prosecution evidence relied largely on the evidence of three eyewitnesses who'd identified Brodsky as a man running away from the scene. One was a barmaid, who'd come off her pub shift early. She'd recognised Brodsky because he'd been an occasional customer of hers. She told the police "I knew him straight away with that bloody great hooter of his." Her evidence had been backed up by two local dog-walkers who'd picked out Brodsky from an identity parade.

Brenda Adams, the victim of the murder, was a 22 year old office worker at the nearby Watney's brewery. She had been dealt a fatal blow to the head. There were signs of sexual interference and her underwear was missing, but she had not been raped. According to her parents, an item or two of jewellery she was never without were missing, but the police concluded that theft was not the main motive for the assault.

Brodsky had shared a flat with a female friend, a fellow Czech musician in a London orchestra, in Barnes. The friendship was supposedly platonic. Brodsky vehemently proclaimed his innocence and had been supported by the flatmate who swore he was incapable of such an act. He had no alibi however and despite the lady's support, the eyewitness evidence held the day and Brodsky was found guilty.

Merlin's involvement had been peripheral. The case had belonged to Chief Inspector George, not one of Merlin's favourite people. Late in the day, as the case was going to trial, George was struck by appendicitis and put out of action temporarily. Merlin was asked to step in and oversee the final stages of the trial procedure from the police side. He had little personal contact with

Brodsky and did not attend every day of the trial, trusting to Inspector George's team, but he'd been there to see the sentencing, which as always was a sombre, unnerving moment for all present. After the judge had finished, a blank-faced Brodsky had been escorted down from the dock to the accompaniment of loud jeers from the relatives of the poor woman who'd been killed.

Merlin was hungry when he got back to the Yard so he was grateful to dip into the biscuit tin Cole brought along with a piping hot cup of tea. Sergeant Sam Bridges arrived moments later. His fair, ruddy features and stocky frame contrasted strongly with his boss's lean build and hawkish good looks.

"Get anywhere in Mayfair, Sergeant?"

"I had a tip-off that a garage owner on Park Lane might be able to provide some useful information, sir, but it was useless. He might have been ready to talk earlier but my guess is someone got to him."

Merlin nodded. "The job has all the hallmarks of Billy Hill's mob. No doubt Hill caught wind the fellow was wobbly and sent someone to put the frighteners on him."

Bridges shrugged, then looked at the large file on Merlin's desk. "Still reading up on the Freeman Bank?"

"Sadly, yes. The AC did us no favours in giving us this."

"Why have we got it, sir? It's not really our sort of case."

"I fear we are the victims of some internal politics the AC's engaging in with the Commissioner. We'll just have to grin and bear it I'm afraid."

Merlin pulled his chair closer to the desk. "I had an odd experience this morning."

'Oh?"

"The raid caught me out and I ended up spending the night here. After the all-clear I went home to grab a few hours of proper rest. On the bus journey I had quite a surprise. You remember the Brodsky case?"

Bridges looked puzzled for a moment. "Something to do with Mortlake?"

"Yes." Merlin reminded Bridges of the case details.

"I remember sir. Fellow got the rope. What about it?"

"The strangest thing. I saw a man who looked exactly like Brodsky get off the bus."

"People do have lookalikes. The wife reckons the man next door to us is the spit of Tommy Handley."

"But this was uncanny. You know what a memory I have for faces, Sergeant. And this man had exactly – and I mean exactly– the same face. The resemblance was so strong I had to wonder if for some reason the execution had not been carried out. I don't know for certain it had. After sentence, the case went back to George when he was back from his appendicitis and I don't actually remember hearing any more."

"We had a lot on our plate at that time, sir. Easy to forget. Shouldn't be hard to confirm though."

"That's the thing. I've just been trying to do that but without success. There are new people in charge at Pentonville Prison, where the execution was due to have taken place. No one has any personal recollection of the event and strangely the paperwork has gone missing. As for DCI George and his people, George himself is away and the others have not been helpful."

"You're bound to get confirmation in due course, sir. There's no way a sentence of that nature wouldn't have been carried out."

Merlin ran a hand through his sleek black hair. "I know you're right but, even so, my interest has been aroused. I think I'd like a word with Brodsky's lady flatmate. Can you track her down for me?"

Ida Samuelson was still living in the ground floor flat she'd shared with Brodsky, in an Edwardian block near Barnes Railway Bridge. Bridges pressed the bell to flat 1, and a short, prim, middle-aged lady with tightly permed dark hair appeared at the door. Merlin made his introductions, and the woman invited the policemen in, an anxious look on her face.

The glass coffee table around which they sat was covered in sheets of music. Miss Samuelson explained that she was learning a new piece by Rachmaninoff. "It's beautiful but it's almost completely new to me and we are due to play it in two nights' time."

"May I ask what your instrument is?" asked Merlin.

The woman stood up and produced a violin from behind her chair. "I can also play the piano and the harp, but the orchestra employs me principally as a violinist."

"Pavel Brodsky was a violinist too, wasn't he?"

Miss Samuelson sat back down and sighed. "He was good enough to be a first violin, but the management never gave him a chance. They had other favourites."

"You and he were close friends?"

"Yes. I miss him very much."

"But you were not…"

"Lovers? No. He was not interested in women in that…in that way if you know what I mean. I told those other policemen that, but they wouldn't believe me. Thought I was just saying anything to save my boyfriend. I said it in court too, but no one believed me. Not even the defence barrister. I could see it in his eyes. A desperate Jew is all he saw. All they all saw. But he was…" She caught her breath then continued for a while extolling Brodsky's virtues and asserting his innocence.

When she'd finished, Merlin asked "If it was not Mr Brodsky who killed the woman on Mortlake Terrace, why were the eyewitnesses so convinced it was him?"

Miss Samuelson pursed her lips. "Excuse my language, Chief Inspector, but that barmaid is a bloody bitch. A Jew-hater too. We used to go to her pub, and she was always very off with us. Then on one occasion, she tried to cheat Pavel out of his change. He made a point of reporting her to the landlord, hence she had a grievance against him. As to the other two eyewitnesses, they were men getting on in years who were influenced by the barmaid's apparent certainty." Miss Samuelson smoothed her skirt. "I'm sorry but you haven't yet told me why you are here. If by any chance the police are thinking of reviewing the case, I'd be happy to repeat all this to any enquiry."

"I don't think I can promise you an enquiry as yet. We just…" Merlin shifted awkwardly in his seat. "It's just…well the main reason we are here is I thought I saw Mr Brodsky yesterday. On a

30

bus. I decided to refresh my memory about the case and…I have to ask…you haven't seen him, have you?"

Miss Samuelson stared back at Merlin in amazement. "I don't believe in ghosts, Chief Inspector."

Merlin got home to his own bed that night and retired early, setting his alarm clock for 6.15. He had an early morning mission. The next day he headed down the King's Road on foot. When he reached Sloane Square, he took up position by a pillar box a short distance from the bus stop where the Brodsky lookalike had alighted the morning before. As he'd hoped, the man got off the bus a short while later. He was dressed as before but was alone this time. The man headed off along Sloane Street and Merlin followed. Halfway up the road he took a left then a right and arrived at a modern block of flats. To the right of the main entrance, there were external stairs descending somewhere and the man disappeared down them.

Merlin stood outside on the opposite pavement wondering what to do. He realised he was not behaving rationally. Once he got back to the Yard, he knew he'd find formal confirmation the Brodsky execution had taken place. What did it matter that the dead man had a double wandering around London? Somehow, however, the coincidence had got under his skin. He couldn't rest until he knew who and what the man was. As he stood pondering, a smartly dressed man wearing a bowler hat came out of the main entrance. He was carrying some rubbish with which he briefly disappeared down a side alley. When he returned empty-handed, he stood for a moment looking officiously up and down the street. Merlin took his chance and crossed the road.

"Are you a porter in this building?"

"I am the Head Porter." The man pronounced stiffly. "Who's asking?"

Merlin produced his warrant card.

The porter relaxed. "The Met, eh? I was on the force myself for a while, er…" he peered at the card, "Chief Inspector Merlin. Gooding's my name. How can I help?"

"I'm interested in the identity of the tenant of this flat." He nodded towards the stairs.

"The basement flat? What's he done?"

"Nothing as far as I know but…but there are reasons I need to learn a little more about him."

"I see. Hush hush stuff, eh? Say no more." He tapped his nose. "The man's called Brown."

"Englishman, is he?"

"No. Foreigner of some sort. Eastern European I think but he's never told me exactly from where. Brown is the name he gave and that's the one on his ID card. Speaks perfect English."

"And do you know what he does for a living?"

"Works in some club up West. Keeps very late hours. I've been told it's not the nicest of clubs if you get my drift. Always amazes me how these places continue to attract customers with all the raids and so on, but I guess it's one way to forget all your troubles. Either way, Mr Brown seems to do quite well out of it. These flats aren't cheap to rent, and he don't seem short of a bob or two. He's got a mate from work who lives further up the road. They have a car which they garage round the corner. Not sure what the exact ownership arrangement is but they use it quite a lot tootling off to places like Richmond Park and so on. Or so Brown tells me." His eyes narrowed. "But maybe they were off spying on munitions factories instead, eh?" Gooding nudged Merlin's arm.

"His friend is a foreigner too?"

"Polish. Very pleasant fellow. Bit of a contrast to Brown who always looks gloomy but then again, I'm not sure his face can look any other way."

"Do you know Mr Brown's Christian name?"

"Andrew."

Merlin let Gooding go, then hovered outside wondering whether he should step down the stairs and confront Andrew Brown. Then he realised he really had nothing with which to confront him. He did now, however, have a name and that was a start. A start to what, though, he didn't know.

Bridges had the expected news back at the Yard. "A lady from Pentonville just rang to confirm that Pavel Brodsky was hanged early on the morning of September 17th. She can send us the paperwork if we want."

"Not necessary, Sergeant. I'll take her word for it."

"So there it is. The man you saw wasn't Brodsky."

Merlin hung up his coat and hat and sat down at his desk. He picked up a pencil and started to doodle on a notepad.

"That's it then, isn't it sir?"

"I have a name for the double, Sergeant. Andrew Brown. English name, but a foreigner according to the porter in his block of flats."

"What does that matter now, sir?"

"Lives off Sloane Street. I walked it back from there. Gave me time to have a think. You see, initially, I had a bee in my bonnet about all this because the resemblance was so striking. Now, I see that the nature of my bee has changed."

Bridges looked bemused. "So what…what 'bee' is it now?"

"Miss Samuelson was so convincing in her defence of Brodsky that I'm almost persuaded he was innocent. If he was innocent another man committed the crime. What if, contrary to the lady's belief, the evidence of the three eyewitnesses was accurate? If they did…"

"They saw a man who looked exactly like Brodsky."

"Yes."

Bridges grinned. "So now you want to reopen the case to see if Brown was the culprit?"

"Just informally. I'd like to take a little time to do some digging."

"You're the boss, sir."

"I know we've got a lot on. You take the lead on everything else for the moment. If there are developments and you need me, I'll drop this."

By the end of the day Merlin knew a good deal about Andrew Brown, including one startling fact. Or was it really so startling? Andrew Brown had been born Ondra Brodsky. A Czech. He could he no one other than Pavel Brodsky's twin brother. He also had a criminal record.

Arriving in England in 1934, a well-qualified engineer, he was offered employment by an industrial equipment company in the Midlands. For whatever reason, he'd changed his name by deed poll in 1935. Then in 1937 he had been charged and convicted of a sexual assault in Coventry and had served nine months in prison. When he came out there was no job waiting for him, but somehow or other he'd landed on his feet. In 1939 he featured for the first time in the files of the West End Central police station as the part-owner of a Soho clip joint. The files showed that minor illegalities at the club were suspected but no action had been taken. There was more, but in summary, it seemed evident to Merlin that Ondra was a much more likely candidate for the assault in Mortlake than Pavel.

Bridges returned to the office just after six. He'd been interviewing employees of the Freeman Bank in the City and gave Merlin a thorough report on progress made. Merlin found it difficult to concentrate on what he was being told. When the Sergeant had finished, Merlin nodded his appreciation, then asked, "Miss Samuelson had a telephone didn't she?"

"She did. I have her number."

"Can you get her for me, please?"

Bridges did as he was asked then handed the receiver to Merlin who got straight to the point. "Are you aware of Mr Brodsky having any close relatives living in England?"

"No. He told me his parents were dead, but he had brothers and sisters living in Czechoslovakia. He'd not heard from any of them for years. God knows what's happening to those poor people now with the Nazis in charge."

"Did he mention that one of his brothers was an identical twin?"

"He did. Before Pavel came to England they fell out over money. He never told me the details. Said they never spoke again."

"So, just to be clear, Pavel was completely unaware that his brother Ondra had been living in England for the past five or six years?"

Miss Samuelson paused briefly before replying. "Well, yes. I think he'd have mentioned it to me if he knew."

"For your information, Miss, not only has his brother been in England but for the past few years he's been in London. I've also been told he enjoyed spending time in places like Richmond, down your neck of the woods. He also served time in an English prison for sexual assault."

There was a longer pause. "But…what are you saying, Chief Inspector? Do you…do you think it might have been him? That Pavel's brother killed poor Brenda Adams?"

"A man looking exactly like Pavel who frequented south west London and has a record for sexual assault. Given your high opinion of Pavel it must be a strong possibility, don't you think?"

"But…"

"Got to go now, Miss Samuelson. I'll keep you posted."

Merlin discussed the phone conversation with Bridges.

"This is all very interesting, sir, but we have no evidence against Brown."

"True but there's nothing to stop me having a chat with the man. I'd like to get him here."

"And if he won't come? You haven't got any grounds for arrest."

"I'll think of something to persuade him."

It was 11.30 the following morning and Merlin sat impatiently at his desk. He had managed to catch Brodsky leaving his flat the previous evening and told the man he wanted to speak to him about his brother. He said some financial questions had arisen and as his closest relative, Brown might be able to help. Nothing untoward. Just a formality. After initially denying he even had a brother, the man had become more accommodating. He was on his way to work and could not speak then, but agreed to come to the Yard at 10.30 in the morning.

"He's not coming, sir, is he?" said Bridges.

Merlin sighed. "Doesn't look like it. Perhaps I should go and get him?"

"If you do it might be a good idea to take Constable Cole with you. Just in case the fellow cuts up rough. I'd come myself, but I've something important on at 12."

"Let's give him fifteen minutes more."

The fifteen minutes passed slowly then Merlin jumped to his feet. "Right, that's it. If you could go and find Cole for me, Sergeant. I…"

The telephone rang and Merlin picked up the receiver. "Yes? Ah, hello Inspector Evans. How's everything at Central?"

"That's what I'm calling about, sir," replied Evans. "We've had an incident on our patch which might be of interest to you. You were asking us questions yesterday about a man called Andrew Brown. Runs a shady Soho club."

"Yes. What about him?"

"He's dead, sir. Someone pulled a gun on him at his club. 3 bullets, one straight to the heart."

Merlin's mind began to race. "But I was only talking to the man last night. He was due at the Yard right now for an interview."

"He won't be giving any more interviews, sir."

Merlin sat back down and shook his head. "What are the circumstances, Inspector? Gangland killing?"

"A possibility, sir, although I'd say it's a little too unprofessional for the professionals, if you follow me. My initial thinking is that the killer was a disgruntled customer. Probably very drunk."

"And most likely a criminal of some kind if he was packing a pistol."

"Just so, sir. Anyway, you know the tricks these places get up to. The girls demanding watered champagne for which the customers are charged a fortune. Everything marked up ten times. It's nothing less than daylight robbery, except it takes place at night. Disturbances are often breaking out in this type of club. Just so happens this disturbance turned out to be fatal."

"Witnesses?"

"Obviously the customers cleared off pronto, as did all of the girls bar one. I have Mr Brown's business partner who's tearing his hair out and largely incoherent. The one girl claims, surprisingly, that the shooter was a woman customer, but she's so

36

drunk I think her evidence is worthless. One of the serving staff says he thought he saw a short man in a hat waving a gun. The three other waiting staff and two bouncers claim to have seen nothing."

"Well…well, thanks for informing me, Inspector. Do you want any help from the Yard?"

"Not at present, sir. I'll keep you posted of course. You're welcome to come and visit the scene if you like. Just let me know."

Merlin put the phone down in a state of shock. "You got the gist of that, Sam?"

"I did, sir."

"Unbelievable." Merlin looked towards the window. The weather had taken a turn for the worse and hailstones were battering the panes. They sat silently for a while, both at a loss for words. Then the telephone rang again.

It was Ida Samuelson. She was in tears and Merlin had to wait a while for her to compose herself.

"I…I had to call you, Mr Merlin. I'm afraid I've found something. Something…something of Pavel's."

"You have?"

"I'm not quite sure how the police missed it. They went over the place with a fine tooth comb at the time of the murder."

"What have you found?"

"I was piling up Pavel's clothes to give to a charity in Barnes and going through the pockets of a jacket when I found it. It wasn't in a main pocket but in a little one behind one of the lapels."

"Strange place to have a pocket."

"Pavel had a lot of quirks like that. He told me it was a good place to hide money in the event of being robbed. The idea had come to him after he'd been attacked once in Czechoslovakia. Anyway, I knew to look for it, unlike your officers."

"And what exactly did you find?"

"A left-luggage ticket. For Waterloo Station."

"I see. You'd like us to go and see what's there?"

"No thank you. I've already done that. It…it…there…there was a small canvas bag. It held two items."

"Yes?"

"A bracelet, a cheap one, and…a…a lady's underwear. A pair of…knickers."

Merlin's mind started to race again. "And was there anything particular about these items?"

"The bracelet had a medallion attached. It bore the name… 'Brenda'."

At the Red Lion, Merlin bought the first round of beer. "The drinks are on me tonight. I've been such an idiot." They ploughed through the crowd and found a quiet corner of the pub. "Clearly, you were right to be sceptical, Sam."

"Not so much sceptical, sir, as…well, thinking we had more pressing things to deal with."

"Delicately put."

"Having said that, the facts of the case have now clearly been laid bare. Without your interest, that might not have happened."

"I'm not so sure about that, Sam."

Bridges shrugged his shoulders. "Poor Miss Samuelson. She thought Pavel wasn't interested in her because he preferred men. Fact was he just didn't fancy her."

"Lucky for her otherwise she might have become a victim of his violent side. As it was, they were able to have a good friendship. Sex isn't everything," said Merlin.

"It was obviously very important to Pavel, at least when it came to pretty young women."

"And their underwear. Mr Freud might have had something interesting to say on the subject."

"Freud?"

"Psychiatrist fellow. Lived up Hampstead way. Died a few months ago. Had a lot to say about sex, I understand. Anyway, there it is. I got it all wrong and I've learned my lesson. If I see the double of a dead man on a bus in the future, I shall just ignore him." Merlin looked away. "And I suppose I have to say a big thank you to Miss Samuelson and the gunslinging madman in Soho for saving me from going off on a wild goose chase."

"You said one of the nightclub witnesses thought the killer was a woman not a man."

38

"So Evans said." Merlin became thoughtful, then shook his head. "Well, that's best left now in the capable hands of the Inspector. It's his case." He took a big gulp of beer then wiped his mouth. "You know, I have to wonder if there's a moral to be drawn from this."

Bridges considered for a moment, then responded "Let sleeping dogs lie, sir?"

Merlin laughed. "Ondra Brodsky was indeed dozing when I first saw him, so that'll do nicely. Well done, Sergeant!" He finished his pint. "I'm thirsty tonight. Ready for another?"

Interview

Can you first please tell us a little more about the series and/or character that your short story is based around?

The main protagonist of my short story is Detective Chief Inspector Frank Merlin, a Scotland Yard detective working in World War Two London. I have written 5 books in my Merlin novel series. 'Let Sleeping Dogs Lie' is the first ever Merlin short story. The books have followed Merlin's police adventures from January 1940 up to, in the fifth book, August 1942. In my short story I have taken a step back in time, in terms of the series, to February 1940, when the Blitz is still in full flow.

The Merlin series features fictional crimes but I make every effort to ensure that the historical background to them is accurate. My first book (The Embassy Murders formerly Princes Gate) is set at the time of what is now known as The Phoney War. Book 2 (In The Shadows of the Blitz formerly Stalin's Gold)) is set in September 1940 against a backdrop of The Battle of Britain and the start of The Blitz. The third Merlin book (The French Spy formerly Merlin At War) takes place in June 1941 and deals with dark dealings among De Gaulle's London-based Free French. A Death In Mayfair, Merlin 4, is set in December 1941, when the Japanese launched their attack on Pearl Harbour, and concerns violent death in the wartime British film industry. My most recent book, Dead In The Water, is set in August 1942, and covers, inter alia, looted art and criminal activity among the recently arrived American troops. The Merlin books include many real characters. Among those who feature are Churchill, Stalin, Goering, Petain and Joseph Kennedy. I make every effort to ensure that their involvement is plausible.

What first attracted you to the period you write about?

My father was in the Navy in the war and some of his service was passed in West Africa. While there he contracted a wasting chest disease from which he eventually died when I was very young. Thus World War Two loomed large in my personal life from an early age. My mother worked in South Wales for the Great Western Railway during the war and used to tell me fascinating stories about her wartime experiences, which included weekend trips up to London to go out on the town at a time when London was being terrorised by Flying Bombs. When I decided to have a go at writing a book, I wanted to write about crime and set it in a historical context. I did some initial research on various periods, including World War Two. When I looked at British wartime criminal activity I discovered that, contrary to what most people think, crime was rampant during the war. The blackout, the black market, substantial gang activity and the booming wartime vice business all contributed to a growth in reported crime of nearly 60 per cent between 1939 and 1945. I decided this was a great period in which to set a detective series.

If there was one moment in history you could witness , featured in one of your novels, what would it be?
I guess it would have to be the Battle of Britain and the Blitz, preferably from a safe vantage point.

What do you think makes so many readers attracted to reading about the Second World War?
The recent passing of Her Majesty the Queen has brought home to people very powerfully that the war generation is on the point of disappearing, and this I think makes people focus in particular on the war years. A number of recent major war anniversaries recently have also served to generate greater interest. Generally, I think historical periods become more fascinating as the events become more distant. With regard to the Second World War, the fact that it was an out and out battle of good and evil, with great heroes and vile villains, makes it particularly riveting and the lives of those who inhabited the period more compelling.

Which other authors, fiction or non-fiction, do you admire who write about the Second World War?

Fiction writers I admire include: Graham Greene, Evelyn Waugh, Elizabeth Bowen, Alan Furst, Philip Kerr, John Lawton, Joseph Heller.

Non-fiction favourites include: Philip Ziegler, Antony Beevor, Ben Macintyre, Juliet Gardiner.

If you could invite three figures from World War Two to dinner, who would they be and why?

I guess it would have to be Churchill, Hitler and Stalin provided I was allowed interpreters. I don't think I really need to say why. If I wasn't allowed interpreters, then Churchill, Dusko Popov (Agent Tricycle) and Paddy Mayne of the SAS. Popov because he was a phenomenally brave and successful spy, and Mayne because he was such an extraordinarily courageous and effective fighting soldier.

What piece of advice would you give to other historical novelists out there, who are just starting out?

Try not to get carried away with the results of your historical research. While readers will generally appreciate learning some interesting new information, don't overdo it. Remember that your primary aim is to entertain.

Can you tell us a little more about your next project?

My next project is Frank Merlin 6. Generally I set a new book some seven to nine months in time after its predecessor. My last book, Dead In The Water, was set in August 1942 and I've chosen to set the new book in May 1943, just when victory in North Africa was making things begin to look a little rosier for the Allies. I don't plan my stories in any great detail. I get most of my plot ideas from the research process. Once I've finished my research and have a few plot subjects in mind, I start writing and see where I go. I am usually three quarters of the way in before I have to start thinking about how the various plot lines should be resolved. So far I have written 40,000 words of the new book, and have 3 plots in progress. I'm still quite a way from knowing how they end!

River-Trent-Bridge, by Alex Gerlis

'When captured German intelligence records were studied after 1945, it was found that almost all of the further 115 or so agents targeted against Britain during the course of the war had been successfully identified and caught. The only exception was an agent who committed suicide before capture.'
MI5

He'd read a number of articles to this effect throughout the 1950s, along with similar references in the growing number of history books now being published about the Second World War.
Every Nazi spy operating in Great Britain was captured...German intelligence was incompetent, their agents all useless...British intelligence 'too smart' for Nazi agents.
He eagerly sought these articles out, devouring every word of them, committing passages to memory before getting rid of them of course, because you couldn't be too careful and even a newspaper article or a history book on a shelf could be regarded as incriminating.

But every reference or quote was a source of considerable comfort, if that was the right word. Reassurance would probably be a better way of putting it.

And they were also a source of wry amusement because when MI5 was quoted as saying that every German spy operating in Great Britain during the war was captured, he knew it made no sense.

After all, they weren't to know what they didn't know, were they?

And he knew that it wasn't true.

***

May 1945
London

VE Day had been the strangest of times for Gottfried Schulte.

The end of the war hadn't come as a surprise of course. Even allowing for the excessively upbeat reporting in the British press, it had been obvious since D-Day the previous June that Germany's defeat was inevitable. He'd arrived in England in early 1943, a month after the defeat at Stalingrad, when the hushed gossip in Berlin was that meant the beginning of the end. But nonetheless, the actual act of surrender had come as a shock and a bitter disappointment.

He was 47 years of age, although according to his British identity he was five years older than that. He was a committed National Socialist, a member of the Nazi Party since he was 28, absolutely dedicated to the cause and his very presence here in London proved he was prepared to lay his life on the line for it.

So, for him, Germany's defeat was devastating, personal and hard to come to terms with.

And yet ... and yet ... he'd have been lying if he didn't acknowledge that the end of the war didn't also come as something of a relief. There'd been no question in his mind that for as long as Germany was at war with Britain, he'd remain an active agent: his loyalty to Hitler was beyond question. For the past two-and-a-bit years he'd willingly operated in enemy territory and every minute of every day was laced with danger. There was no moment when he could feel relaxed or not under threat of capture. He rarely slept for more than an hour at a time, always alert to any sound or even the absence of it. The tension of operating like this for so long had begun to take its toll. He'd lost a considerable amount of weight, appeared to have aged by ten years and smoked at least thirty cigarettes a day.

But as he walked among the vast crowds jostling in the streets of London, he realised that he now felt more relaxed. Not that he was no longer in danger, but the fact that his mission had ended with the war meant he could now concentrate on his own safety.

He'd long decided he'd have to remain in England. There were too many people in Germany who knew his true identity and were aware of what he was up to. He'd stay in England, dispose of his Andrew Holt identity and start using a new one. He'd leave London. He'd yet to decide where to go.

But first he had to deal with the one person in England who knew about him.

***

November 1944
London & Bedford

He was his radio man, his point of contact in England, through whom he communicated with Berlin and as far as he was aware the only person on these shores who knew anything about him; it took Gottfried Schulte the best part of five months to find out where he lived.

His own code name was Bridge and the radio man's was Trent. Trent was both his lifeline and his Achilles Heel. If Trent was ever caught – and radio operators were especially vulnerable – then his own existence could be exposed. But he knew he had to work with Trent, who provided him with funds and messages from Berlin, and a few words of encouragement each time they met. Trent was clearly very good at his job, but Bridge knew little about him other than what he observed: a short man possibly in his sixties, invariably wrapped in a shabby, oversized raincoat and – as far as he could tell – English, though there could have been a hint of an accent. Their meetings were short and business-like. They rarely indulged in talk about the war or their part in it.

They contacted each other through postcards in the windows of newsagents in the Holborn, Kings Cross area. There were a dozen newsagents that they used which mean that he had to ensure that walked past each newsagent at least every three or four days and he assumed Trent did the same.

Cleaner needed Tuesdays. Usual rates.

This would mean Trent wanted to see him on Wednesday and 'cleaner' indicated outside the laundry on Eversholt Street and 'usual rates' meant usual time.

By his third meeting with Trent in the early summer of 1943, Bridge came to the conclusion he had to know more about the only person who was aware of his presence in England.

It took him six months, a careful, laborious process which started with him following Trent for a short distance after their meetings, then picking up his route later on. His big breakthrough came on a scorching day in August when Trent seemed to be moving more slowly and taking fewer precautions and he was able to follow him to St Pancras station, where Bridge decided not to push his luck and returned to his bedsit in Crouch End.

He thought about it that evening and decided that Trent probably commuted into London through St Pancras, and his journey to and from work most probably took him past the various newsagents they used for their messages. Certainly, their meetings tended to be around lunchtime or after five o'clock.

Bridge spent a few mornings at St Pancras watching the trains depositing the office workers and eventually spotted Trent coming off a train that, as far as he could tell, had started at Leicester. After that it was a matter of time: watching him leave in the evenings and then joining the train, and in early October he worked out his destination was definitely a town called Bedford. After that, it took a few more careful weeks. Trent seemed less cautious once he left the train in Bedford and although Bridge still had to be very careful, he got there in the end: the bus he took from outside the station, the stop he got off at, the five-minute walk down a main round road before turning into a tree-lined street which reminded him of parts of Hamburg and where the small but neat semi-detached houses were arranged behind immaculately-tended hedges.

It was straightforward enough after that to establish that the only residents of number 43 were Reginald Richard Swann and Marjorie Anne Swann.

And that was all Gottfried Schulte needed to know.

For the time being, at any rate.

***

ACTION THIS DAY

<u>September 1945</u>
Bedford

'River knows all about you. Trust me, I can tell you where to find River!'

Except it didn't sound nearly anything as coherent as that. Trent delivered the words with Gottfried Schulte's hands wrapped around his neck and as they tightened the man's face bulged and turned red and the words came out in an inarticulate splutter, punctuated by croaking noises and a lot of saliva.

...where ... to...find ... River...

It was the first mention he'd ever heard of River but who or what River was wasn't his priority at that moment, which was something he was to come to profoundly regret. His priority was to keep a firm grip on the man's neck and tighten it, and this was proving to be particularly difficult, especially wearing his leather gloves, despite the man being smaller and older than him.

Eventually, he adjusted his body, shuffling up so he was astride the man's chest, his knees pinning his arms down so that now he could force his thumbs deep into the man's Adam's Apple, using the whole weight of his body.

Reginald Richard Swann began to make a croaking sound and Bridge must have relaxed his grip because suddenly the man spoke.

'Um Himmels willen!'

For heaven's sake!

The man had spoken in a perfect German accent. Bridge had never suspected and stared at him in disbelief, momentarily wondering if he ought to stop and the man must have sensed his hesitation because he lifted his head and even smiled and spluttered 'Ich bitte dich!' – *I beg you* – but this plea had the effect of making Bridge realise he needed to get on with it. So he tightened his grip, and after what seemed an age the man stopped moving.

He watched as a trickle of blood ran from his nose and joined another one from his mouth. His eyes were so bloodshot they were almost entirely red. Holt paused for a minute or so while he caught

47

his breath, then removed the man's tie and stuffed it in his mouth before covering his face with his jacket, though not before removing his wallet. He took out two one-pound notes and the three ten-shilling ones, leaving the identity card and a few tickets and receipts. He did wonder about the identity card: it was always handy to have one extra identity, but he wanted this to look like a plain robbery.

Common and garden, as the English liked to term it. A common and garden robbery gone wrong.

And then he waited.

Marjorie Anne Swann returned an hour later, as he'd expected, letting herself in through the back door, cheerfully announcing she was home and then fussing around in the kitchen as she put away the shopping. He waited until she came in the small hallway, where he'd removed the lightbulb and closed the doors from it so it was dark.

He killed her far more quickly, grabbing her head and twisted it sharply, breaking her neck. He moved both bodies upstairs, placing them next to each other on their bed and covering them with blankets and then he went downstairs to tidy things up, putting the bulb back on in the hallway and drawing all the curtains.

And then he began to search the house, opening every drawer and cupboard, moving furniture, lifting rugs and carpet, checking floorboards, going through all the papers and documents. He climbed into the small roof space and searched every inch of it. It took him five hours and by the time he'd finished he was satisfied there was nothing incriminating in the house. Trent had obeyed his orders.

He had no idea where he kept his radio transmitter or whether it had been destroyed but even if it still existed and could be linked with Reginald Richard Swann, Reginald Richard Swann couldn't be linked with Gottfried Schulte, though of course, Gottfried Schulte had been Andrew Holt since he arrived in this country.

But not for much longer.

He'd stay in the house in Bedford overnight and leave the following day, and once he'd collected his few possessions from his bedsit in London he'd move on.

And he'd leave Andrew Holt behind. Harold Anthony Scott would be his new identity, a rock solid one he'd spent months creating.

***

November 1960
Leeds

Harry Scott had done well. Since disposing of Andrew Holt fifteen years earlier he'd rarely given much thought to Gottfried Schulte. He'd moved around the country for a while after leaving London in 1945, ending up in Leeds in 1949 and getting a job as an electrician with the newly formed Yorkshire Electricity Board.

He'd assumed he'd move on after a few years but somehow it never happened and the longer he remained there, the less he felt the need to move. He felt established in Leeds, he was safe there, he fitted in, and he liked the city, where people were friendly but not too nosey and were accepting of others as long as they were no problem to them.

It was a place where not too many questions were asked and that suited him perfectly. He did well at the YEB, becoming a senior foreman but avoiding the chance to become a manager. He didn't fancy the interviews he'd have to go through. His didn't want people probing into his background.

He was able to afford a small terrace house in the Scarcroft area in the north east of the city. It was quite close to the YEB's head office and ideally, he'd have liked to have lived in Roundhay, but there were too many Jews there for his liking. In the early 1950s, there were times when he thought about visiting Germany and on one occasion, he even picked up a brochure from Thomas Cook's in the city centre, but he soon realised it was a crazy idea.

What would he do in Germany? Return to Hamburg and visit places he grew up and where friends and family lived? Go to Berlin where he'd lived and worked for so long and where he'd been recruited? Heidelberg, where he'd been at university? It was, he concluded, a crazy idea. He had no idea who'd survived the war, but the risk of someone recognising him was too great.

And if he avoided the places he knew, then what? He'd be a stranger in his own land, angry at what Germany had become, bitter at those who colluded in the defeat of Third Reich.

So, Harold Anthony Scott stayed where he was. He never visited London again, of course went nowhere near Bedford, and because of his codename and that of his radioman – Trent and Bridge –avoided the city of Nottingham, just in case.

His pride and joy was his Morris Minor, bought on a scheme through his work and which he lovingly maintained. On his holidays he'd drive north, sometimes to the Lake District, other times to Northumbria or into Scotland. He stayed at bed and breakfast places and went for long walks, enjoying the solitude and taking not a little comfort and quite a lot of pride in the fact that he'd survived.

He'd never been caught.

No one suspected him and there was no reason why that would change.

But things did change.

Harold Anthony Scott had been born in March 1895, which meant that in March 1960 he'd reached the age of retirement of 65, an event most men he knew looked forward to but one which left him bereft.

He wasn't ready to retire. Gottfried Schulte was only 62 so he'd plenty of working years left in him, and more to the point, what was he going to do? He enjoyed his work and it filled his time and enabled him to have a group of colleagues with whom he could have things in common and be friendly, without them being actual friends and all the risks that entailed.

He did ask if he could stay on, but was told that was not an option. There were drinks with a few colleagues in his manager's office on a Friday afternoon and the presentation of a watch. The following week he collected his state pension of just under three pounds a week for the first time and the week after that he received his £1 a week pension from the YEB. He knew he could get by fine on that, and keep his car running, and he'd pick up the odd bit of electrical work, but what was he to do with all that time?

He turned, as so many men he knew did, to the pub. The Crown and Dragon wasn't the nearest pub, which was why he chose it. He'd order a pint of bitter, which was not a drink he was too fond of but it would have looked odd had he ordered anything else and the one thing he avoided was looking odd.

The Crown and Dragon couldn't have been more pleasant. It was a warm and inviting place with a couple of snugs leading off the main bar area and each of them had a log fire and a couple of tables where people either sat on their own or with companions. And there was an etiquette about the place which suited him fine: you could sit on your own and not be bothered or chat with someone, passing the time of day and after a couple of hours feel you'd had company. He realised he'd been quite lonely and the pub, to an extent, filled the role previously occupied by work.

They'd talk about football or the weather or the news, avoiding expressing too much of an opinion. There was a group of men of a similar age who came in most evenings around six thirty after their tea and he started to sit with them. On any given evening four of them would come and he became particularly friendly with a couple of them, certainly on first name terms.

There was Fred who'd worked for the Gas Board, Trevor who'd been a foreman in a warehouse and Walter who, as far as he could tell, had been some sort of travelling salesman. Over time, Walter was the one he became most friendly with. They seemed to have things in common. Walter was also unmarried, more reserved, not that much of a drinker and also, he suspected, somewhat lonely too. And Fred had mentioned that Walter was a relative newcomer to the group, like Harry.

The two men became quite friendly, meeting in the pub before any of the others turned up and comfortable enough in each other's company not to feel obliged to talk all the time.

As the summer of 1960 turned to autumn and the days became shorter and the evenings darker and colder Walter became increasingly maudlin. Life had become difficult, he confided. He'd had a difficult war. He was estranged from his family.

Harry Scott didn't ask many questions because he didn't want to be asked any in return, but he did try to be sympathetic. Though he did begin to feel slightly uneasy, especially after one evening when the foul weather meant that none of their other usual companions turned up and he was stuck with Walter all evening. The conversation turned to money and he admitted that with his pensions and his savings he was quite comfortable. Walter said he'd been unlucky with money and maybe Harry could lend him some money because 'a Jew in Chapeltown' had swindled him. He'd then turned to face Harry full on and leaned closer to him and then said, 'you'll know what I mean.' Scott was so thrown by that he nodded, then took out his wallet and handed two ten-shilling notes to Walter, and said he hoped this would tide him over. Walter took the money quickly and said it would certainly help.

The same happened a week later, Walter promising to pay back the money in due course but asking if it was possible to borrow another pound, because he was hopeful of getting his money back and once again, he was sure Harry would understand.

Harry Scott was so uneasy now that for a few days he avoided the Crown and Dragon. When he returned, claiming a heavy cold had kept him away, Walter seemed put out by his absence and said there'd been a setback with getting his money, but if he could see his way to lending him five pounds then he could afford to see a solicitor and he'd definitely succeed then.

He brought the money the following evening, but avoided the pub for another week after that and had pretty much decided never to return to the Crown and Dragon again. He'd write the money off as a bad debt, a price worth paying to never see Walter again.

***

It was a vicious Wednesday night in November when there was a knock at his door just after eight o'clock. When he opened it, Harry didn't recognise the hunched, drenched figure on the doorstep. By the time he realised it was Walter, the man was already in the hallway, and Harry was in shock because he had no idea he knew where he lived.

Walter said nothing as he took off his cap and still wearing his shoes and wet raincoat walked into the living room and sat himself on the sofa. Harry was so unused to visitors, he had no idea what to say or what to do, but then Walter told him to sit down an uncharacteristically firm manner.

It sounded like an order.

Harry muttered something about the debt now being seven pounds and if he could see his way to …

'It's not about the debt.' Walter looked around the room, nodding his head as if to signify his approval. 'You've done well for yourself, haven't you?'

'Thank you, I …'

'They always said you were smart.'

Harry felt his breathing become shallower and his throat tighten. There was an undeniable menace about Walter's tone and demeanour.

'But not that smart, eh?'

'I'm not sure I'm following you Walter, I …'

'You were Bridge. The man I assume you killed in Bedford in 1945 was Trent. But if you'd been as smart as they said you were, you'd have known there were three of us: River, Trent, Bridge. Who do you think gave Bridge his orders, eh?'

'River?' The word barely came out. His mouth was unbearably dry and he felt dizzy. He recalled Trent's desperate words: *River knows all about you.*

Walter leaned over, smiling, his hand outstretched. 'Indeed. I can't tell you how pleased I am to have finally found you.'

Interview

Can you first please tell us a little more about the series and/or character that your short story is based around?

The main character in my short story is Gottfried Schulte – codenamed Bridge, a German spy operating in Britain during the Second World. The story is about how he remains undetected when the war ends and what he does to ensure he's not caught. I've always been intrigued by the accepted line that all German spies operating in the United Kingdom during the Second World War were caught. To me, there seems to be a lack of logic in saying something so unequivocal, because we don't know what we don't know: a German spy who was so smart that they were never caught was highly unlikely to pop up many years later and tell their story. It's a hard subject for historians without any proof, but more fertile ground for a novelist.

What first attracted you to the period you write about? How do you approach researching your novels?

I covered the 50th anniversary of D-Day for the BBC in 1994 and became fascinated with the role that the deception operation had in the success of the Allied landings and their eventual victory in the Battle of Normandy. This gave me the initial idea for the plot in my first novel, *The Best of Our Spies*. The success of that book made me realise that the Second World War espionage fiction genre was one I wanted to write about. There is so much material from that war, not just the events in it but also the locations and the people, all of which I hope I use to create a credible and authentic atmosphere that people can relate to today. My research is quite thorough: I'll visit the key locations, study the relevant contemporary maps, interview people with a contemporary knowledge and read the key books on the subject.

If there was one moment in history you could witness, featured in one of your novels, what would it be?

ACTION THIS DAY

There's very little in what I write about that could be described as 'uplifting' or which I could say I'd want to witness without it appearing to be in bad taste. Having said that, the liberation of some of the cities must have been extraordinary and so being in Paris from 19th - 25th August 1944 must have been very powerful. I'm a great admirer of Vasily Grossman's journalism, and while it would have been the most dreadful experience, being with the Red Army as they liberated Eastern Europe from the hell of the Nazi occupation would have been a profound experience. Grossman's account of the liberation of the Treblinka death camp is one of the most powerful examples of journalism I have ever read.

What do you think makes so many readers attracted to reading about the Second World War?

I think one reason it continues to be so popular is that it works well in story terms, in that the Second World War has a defined beginning, middle and end – which means it fits well into a story's structure. Another reason could be the very dramatic nature of the war: the events were so appalling that in many respects it hasn't been surpassed since then. And then the war was perhaps the first one properly recorded in terms of pictures and film, so people can relate to it.

Which other authors, fiction or non-fiction, do you admire who write about the Second World War?

Fiction authors on the Second World War is a tricky one because I feel I have to avoid reading too much fiction on the subject as I'm wary of inadvertently picking up plots or characters. Having said that, I'm a big fan of Alan Furst: I've read all of his books and I'd say that his early ones in particular inspired to write about this era. I'm attracted by the way one can marry plot, characters, real events and places and in doing so, create an atmosphere that in some way gets close to those times. I read so much non-fiction from this period that in some ways it would be invidious to single out one or two authors, not least because I'm bound to offend other writers in this edition. Antony Beevor's books on the Second World War are outstanding – *Stalingrad* and *Berlin* are classics. I look for books that manage to get behind the obvious military angles and manage to tell the story of what day-to-day life was like. Roger Moorhouse's *Berlin at War* is a good example of this. Ian Ousby's *Occupation* was a very original approach to looking at France during the war.

If you could invite three figures from WW2 to dinner, who would they be and why?

As interesting as they'd be from a journalist's or historian's point of view, I'd avoid any of the Germans involved in the running of the war: I wouldn't want to share a table with them. I'm going to invite: Jean Moulin, the leader of the French resistance, murdered by the Gestapo in July 1943. He was captured by the Gestapo in Lyon the month before and was the person behind the unification of the resistance, turning it into what became an effective organisation. I'd also invite Vasily Grossman, mentioned above. He was an acclaimed novelist and an outstanding war reporter for the Red Army newspaper. My third guest would be Marek Edelman, who was one of the leaders of the Jewish Fighting Organisation in the 1943 Ghetto Uprising, and one of its few survivors. After the war, Edelman became a leading cardiologist in Poland, despite coming from a very humble background and having been orphaned at a young age. If any of them were unable to make it, I'd invite Viktor Frankl, the eminent psychiatrist, survivor of Auschwitz, and author of the remarkable *Man's Search for Meaning*.

What piece of advice would you give to other historical novelists out there, who are just starting out?

Don't think that you're a historian, you're a novelist. By all means, try and be as accurate as possible about the historical context in which your book is set, but don't pretend the book is a history one. The key is to tell a story well, with a plausible plot, credible characters and plenty of twists and storylines to ensure the readers turn the page. Don't worry too much about the ending: I never know my endings until very late in the book – I think if you've got a good enough story and strong enough characters, then the ending will develop naturally.

Can you tell us a little more about your next project?

It's a four-book series starting in the mid-1930s and ending in 1956 (there's a clue). The plan is to cover the rise of the Nazis, Stalin's purges and Soviet espionage, the Second World War and then the Cold War, with one main character, a theme of divided and shifting loyalties and treason – with the mystery of who is the powerful traitor wreaking havoc in London only being resolved in the final book.

The Bridge at Siebenhäuscrn, by Allan Martin

Highland Light Infantry. The words conjure up lithe and lightly-armed young men blending into the colours and contours of the land as they creep noiselessly towards the unsuspecting enemy. At the last moment, they rise as one, calling the fearsome slogan of their clan. The defenders panic, fire a wild and inaccurate volley, drop their weapons and take to their heels.

Sadly, the reality is better captured by the words 'cannon fodder.' In the course of the Jacobite risings, the highland warrior was seen as a threat to the British state. A convenient solution to the problem was to make use of his bravery and fighting skills in places far from home, and in situations from which he was unlikely to return. General Wolfe's comment – "No great mischief if they fall" – is well-known. The highlanders were regarded by the rulers of the British Empire in the same way as Indian troops: brave and expendable. In 1940 it was the highland regiments which were chosen to shield the fleeing British Army as it abandoned its French and Belgian allies to run for the beaches of Dunkirk. The highlanders sustained heavy casualties, and those who survived spent the rest of the war in German concentration camps.

My grandfather, Hector Darroch, served in a highland regiment in that war. He joined up in 1942, and since he was the manager of a small branch of the Commercial Bank of Scotland, he was considered officer material. His action began, after training in Scotland, in 1944 with the Normandy landings, and continued into the advance across Northern France and into Germany itself. He was by turns promoted to Lieutenant, then Captain; and not being one of the toffs, that's as high as he would ever be allowed to go.

As boys, my brother and I were keen to hear of his exploits against the Jerries. You could still get comics then featuring handsome commandoes with impeccable accents – "I say, Ginger, let's see off these chaps now, shall we?" – and overweight Germans called von Gherkin who habitually called out "Donner

58

und Blitzen!" and addressed each captured commando as "Englischer Schweinhund!" But Grandpa was resolutely silent on the matter. He simply said he didn't dwell on the past, and no amount of pleading would move him.

Forty years later, with children of my own, long after he had passed away, I began to research the family history, and naturally wanted to find out more about Grandpa's wartime experiences. I was lucky enough to find on eBay a copy of a history of his regiment during World War Two. *March Into Germany* was written by a retired colonel, and published in 1962. The book was not supplied with an index, but I found Captain Darroch mentioned on one page near the middle of the volume. The regiment had, by February 1945, reached the river Rhine at Dreieckendorf, and were given the task of capturing the bridge which crossed the river to the little town of Siebenhäusern.

After heavy fighting, the defensive works at Dreieckendorf were captured. However the eastern end of the bridge was also defended, by solid concrete pillboxes from which fire could be sprayed across the only means of approach, that is, the road across the river. For two days the highlanders repeatedly attempted to take the fortifications by a frontal assault, but without success, sustaining heavy casualties at each attempt. On the third day, however, an assault in the early morning led by Captain Darroch, again with the loss of many men, succeeded in overrunning the enemy positions, and twenty-six German prisoners were taken. The regiment could now proceed on the road to its target, the city of Bremen. I read the entire book, but my grandfather received no further mention.

I determined to visit the scene of these events, and last October, with the children at university, I booked my wife and myself into the Gasthof zum Brückkopf in Siebenhäusern. Gisela is herself German – we met when I was on a walking tour of Thuringia – and is always up for a visit, although this was a part of the country she did not know.

Our walk across the bridge on the evening of our arrival confirmed that this was the same bridge that had stood in 1945. The heavy stone piers were clearly visible, above each one an arch with twin towers, miraculously preserved, or faithfully restored, and even the wrought-iron balustrade remained. Of course, there were no remains of the defensive works which had stood at either end of the structure. In the 1960s the autobahn was constructed, crossing the river a few miles further north, bypassing both Dreieckendorf and Siebenhäusern. Dreieckendorf had been badly damaged in the fighting, and had lost most of its historic buildings; by contrast, in Siebenhäusern much of the old town centre had survived, and was painstakingly renovated, so that one could almost imagine it as it had been back in 1945.

The next day a visit to the town museum confirmed what we'd seen. Old photographs of the town before the war showed how painstaking had been the refurbishment. There were also shots of the town after its capture by the allies. Remarkably little damage had been done, and most of this by artillery firing across the river. The museum display said merely that the bridge had been taken by Allied forces on 17th February 1945. The young woman at the counter could add no further details. The booklet on sale at the museum on the town's history said little more – only that the defence of the bridge against the Allies had continued for several days before the defenders finally surrendered.

Over the next two days we explored the surrounding area. The weather was dry but cold. We got to know the hotel proprietor, Herr Dreschler, a rotund and jovial man looking every inch the jolly innkeeper. In the course of one conversation, I told him why we'd come to his town in particular, and that we'd not been able to get much more information about what had happened that day in 1945.

"Ach," he said, "But you should have asked me this as soon as you arrived. We have still here in the town a witness to those events. Andreas Reilitz. He was a teenager at the time, and worked in the inn here for my grandfather. He's old now, but still in good health for his age. He comes here regularly, around seven. I'll introduce you to him."

That evening, we ate in the hotel. Herr Dreschler directed us to a table near the wide fireplace, where a log fire crackled and gave out more heat than was comfortable for us. "You'll have to sit here," he said, "Andreas feels the cold."

At seven on the dot, the door opened, and an old man entered. I guessed he'd once been tall, now shrunken by age, and also by a slight stoop. He was thin and his face bore many wrinkles, but his eyes were bright and his hair was white, and he walked with the aid of a stick. Herr Dreschler met him at the door and spoke quietly to him. He looked sharply in our direction, examining us both, then made his way towards our table.

"*Guten Abend*," he greeted us politely, "You are interested in the crossing of the bridge in 1945?"

Gisela, whose German is naturally better than mine, explained why we were interested, that my grandfather Captain Darroch had been present, but we knew little about what had actually happened.

"So, you are from *Schottland*? Then you are welcome. I will join you." He sat down at the table, with his back to the fire. "My back grows stiff," he said, "I need to keep it heated."

I rose to buy him a drink, but he waved me back to my seat. "Please, sit down. Franz will bring our drinks. I am happy to honour the grandson of Captain Darroch." He smiled. "And I think, after your Brexit, you will need your money more than I, eh?"

Herr Dreschler now appeared with a dark brown bottle and three shot glasses. The label read '*Klettmeier Pflaumenschnapps.*'

"Plum brandy, from a local estate," said Herr Reilitz, as he poured us each a full measure of the golden liquid. "It is of exceptional quality, and so warming in the winter months. *Prost!*" He smelled the liquid, then took a sip, let it roll round in his mouth and swallowed. "In my youth," he said, "I would drain the glass in one drink. Today I enjoy the taste as well as the warmth. Well, now I'm ready to tell you what happened back then."

Gisela held her glass up to him and took a tiny sip. "*Sehr gut*," she said, nodding. I smelt the brandy. More than a hint of plums, but with depth rather than sweetness. Grown-up plums, I thought, took rather a large sip and rolled the liquid round my mouth. The heaviness reminded me of well-aged Islay whisky, though the taste was different – who can describe the taste of the best spirits – and when I swallowed, the power of it made me clench my teeth, as the heat worked its way into my chest.

"So," said Herr Reilitz, "You like our old *schnapps*?"

"*Ja, ja,*" I gasped, "*Auch für mich, es ist sehr gut. Wie ein alter whisky.*"

"*Das ist ja so,*" he smiled again. "And now I tell the story. Some of this I witnessed myself, the rest I heard soon afterwards from those who were present. I was fourteen at the time. Too young to be fighting, although I wanted to. I was working in the inn here, for Franz's grandfather, old Herr Dreschler. My mother had taken my sisters into the country, to the farm of her cousin. My father was a mechanic in the Luftwaffe, stationed near Kiel. Mother wanted me to come to the farm too, but *Opa* – my grandfather – told her not to worry, he would keep me out of trouble. And so he did. The bunker behind the inn was always ready for us to dash into at, how would you say, a moment's notice. And, as you see, I am still in one piece." He took another sip, and we followed suit. I was beginning to like the stuff now.

"You must first know that the bridge here was well-defended. *Hauptmann* – I think that is the equivalent of your Captain – *Hauptmann* Klettmeier was in command. Yes, you recognise the name. His family owned a vineyard and orchard near the town. A good man, and no lover of the Nazis, but he felt it his duty to fight for his country. He'd been wounded on the Eastern Front, invalided home, and recruited again for defensive duties here. He was an astute commander; he used the teenagers, cripples and old men under his command well, placed them cleverly and made sure the defences were in good repair. He advised the high command that the most sensible measure would be to blow up the bridge. His suggestion was denounced as defeatism. 'Soon the forces of the Reich will flood across the bridge to drive the enemy back towards the sea,' he was told. But he knew the war was already lost.

"We could see and hear the fighting across the river in Dreieckendorf. The British were cautious; they made no attempt to attack until the south side of the river was completely pacified. On the morning of the fifteenth, they attempted to cross the bridge. The attack was suicidal – their leaders were merely throwing men at us to see what the defences were like. So many lives thrown away when anyone with a pair of Zeiss binoculars could have worked it out. They needed tanks, but they didn't have any. So it was a little like World War One – men running at machine guns and barbed wire. They had a few howitzers, which lobbed shells at random into the town, causing some damage, but making little impact on the defensive positions. Most of the townsfolk had moved out into the countryside until the fighting would pass.

"On the second day, this scene of pointless bloodshed was repeated. They had learned nothing. Did they hope our men would get tired of killing, or run out of ammunition? Such a tragic waste of life. Many brave young men died on the bridge. They didn't even attempt to retrieve the bodies.

"The first two attacks had commenced at three o'clock in the afternoon, when they hoped the sun would be behind them. But the days were cloudy, so there was no sense in that either. Maybe some general who remembered what he'd done in the first war ordered it. So the defenders waited again for the next attack. But before it was due, at 1.30, something curious happened. I was watching from one of the upper windows of the inn, which had, because of its location behind the defensive works, suffered so far only superficial damage.

"We heard first of all the bagpipes, piercing and haunting, an ancient summoning. Looking across, we saw walking onto the bridge three men in kilts. The leader was an officer, carrying a white flag, beside him walked a younger man. And behind them strode the piper. He played a march, but with a mournful aspect. *The Battle of the Somme*, it was called, we learned later. The man who wrote it was killed in that same battle one week later. A reminder of earlier pointless killing, eh?" He nodded to himself, and took another drink.

"*Hauptmann* Klettmeier was familiar with the rules of war. After making sure that they were all unarmed, he permitted them to cross without hindrance. The officer – this was your grandfather, Captain Darroch – asked to speak with the leader of the defenders. And where did the meeting take place, but here in our inn! So, between serving beer and sausages with rye bread, I was able to watch, and listen. It turned out that the younger man, a junior officer, was a fluent German-speaker, and Captain Darroch used him as an interpreter.

"He explained to *Hauptmann* Klettmeier the general position along the Rhine, that the British and Americans had already crossed at several points, and would eventually reach Siebenhäusern from the North. Tanks were also being brought up to force the bridge. If the Germans continued to resist, many men would die on both sides and the town would suffer much damage. And all for nothing.

"*Hauptmann* Klettmeier knew little of the strategic position; he had only been given orders to defend the bridge to the last man. But he had heard the rumours which swept along the river like gulls riding the wind. All of them bad. He asked many questions, all of which were answered freely by Captain Darroch. He did not need to invent anything; it was clear the Allies were advancing inexorably, with forces greater than ours. The *Hauptmann* could have used this information to perhaps hold the bridge for another two days, or he could have passed it back to his superiors.

"He did neither. He was a good judge of a man, and realised Captain Darroch was being honest with him, that it was not a trick. He also loved this place and its people, and did not wish to see further destruction and killing. He offered therefore to surrender the bridge, to open it to the British at nine o'clock the following morning. Captain Darroch agreed. The junior officer was sent back across the bridge with a message to the regiment's colonel. Captain Darroch remained to work out the exact terms. He produced from his capacious pocket a half-bottle of whisky and suggested a toast. Naturally *Hauptmann* Klettmeier responded by calling for the best *schnapps* from his own estate, a fine bottle from before the war, made from pears. There was a sense of relief, that here in Siebenhäusern the war would end peacefully, without further killing.

"About half an hour later the junior officer, Lieutenant McTaggart, returned with a letter for Captain Darroch. He read it, then put it in his pocket without a word. 'Headquarters have approved our arrangement,' he announced. We all cheered. The atmosphere in the inn became more relaxed; the piper played tunes for us, and old Johann Bauer fetched his accordion. Lieutenant McTaggart sang songs in Gaelic that made us weep although we didn't understand a word. We all joined in singing *Lilli Marlene*, and then *Auld Lang Syne*. As the darkness began to fall, the three Scottish soldiers returned to their lines across the bridge.

"Next morning a different officer came to accept the formal surrender. Naturally, *Hauptmann* Klettmeier asked where Captain Darroch was. He learned that he had been arrested for insubordination as soon as he had returned to his lines. Apparently, he had no orders from his colonel to arrange any surrender. The colonel had planned further suicidal assaults on the bridge, but could do nothing once the ceasefire was agreed. However, despite the successful outcome of the talks, he took out his spite on Captain Darroch. The other officer, a friend of Darroch's, regarded the colonel's behaviour as despicable.

"All passed peacefully as arranged, and, as they say, for us the war was over. We were thankful it was the British to whom the town had been surrendered, that our homes were on the Rhine, and not the Oder. We had heard of the fate of towns in the east, when they had been taken by the Russians. The butchery and rape and looting, like something out of the Thirty Years War. Nevertheless, it was some years before life returned to normal, and we worked hard to rebuild our lives.

"Imagine our surprise when, maybe four or five years after the war had ended, Captain Darroch came with his wife to visit us. They stayed in this very inn, although Franz will tell you that the facilities are much improved since then. He worked, I think, for a bank in Scotland, and did not wish to be addressed by his former military title.

"*Herr* Darroch told us the rest of the story. He was arrested for negotiating with the enemy without authorisation, and was sent for court-martial. The war was still on, and so the prosecutors demanded death by firing squad, as a warning to others. The colonel himself intended to be the main witness for the prosecution. However, the proceedings were reported by other officers to General Montgomery, the supreme commander. Although, naturally, he disapproved of insubordination, the general saw the sense in negotiating a solution which would avoid the wastage of his soldiers' lives. He ordered the charges to be quashed, and Captain Darroch to be transferred to another posting away from the fighting. He spent the rest of the war in charge of a refugee camp not far north of Bremen. And then returned to his bank."

He raised his glass to us. "I toasted your noble grandfather then, and I toast him again now. *Prost!*" This time he drained the glass in one.

The end of the tale was greeted by sustained applause. We hadn't realised that gradually everyone in the room had joined in listening to the story.

Back in our bedroom, I looked again at the regimental history. My grandfather's part in the crossing had been entirely falsified. The writer preferred to tell a tale of brave men dying needlessly for their country, rather than of sensible men talking together to find their way out of a difficult situation, without further loss of life. Fake history. The myth of glorious death had to be sustained, ready for the next war.

Interview

Can you first please tell us a little more about the series and/or character that your short story is based around?

The story is completely fictitious, as are the places mentioned. The character of Captain Darroch is loosely based on my Estonian detective, Jüri Hallmets, who had fought in the Estonian War of Independence (1918-1920). However, my father, as an officer in the Highland Light Infantry, was involved in the crossing of the Rhine in 1944. Like Captain Darroch, he would say nothing of his experiences during the war. He was, at the end of the war, in command of a refugee camp, and after the war returned to his job as a branch manager for an insurance company.

What first attracted you to the period you write about?

Estonia in the 1930s had only recently achieved independence, was running its own affairs and was discovering its own identity. There was a great sense of liberation, but at the same time the clouds were gathering. A small country, coveted by both Hitler's Germany and Stalin's Russia, was, in the end, bound to lose. A time and a place so different from our own.

How do you approach researching your novels?

Historical novels have to feel real, and characters as well as places and historical events have to be authentic. That involves a lot of research. Regular trips to Estonia enabled me to visit locations used, and thoroughly study the background. I also learned to read Estonian, as few of the sources for Estonian history are in English. A lot of effort, but certainly worth it. The big danger for a writer of historical fiction is that you find the research so interesting that you want to pass it all on to the reader. You have to limit the information you supply to what will enable the reader to understand what's driving the narrative.

ASPECTS OF HISTORY

If there was one moment in history you could witness, featured in one of your novels, what would it be?

The period immediately after the Estonian War of Independence, 1920-1921, when Estonia was creating itself as an independent state, with major social and economic changes, and enormous optimism. An exciting time when everything was possible.

What do you think makes so many readers attracted to reading about the Second World War?

In contrast to the moral ambiguity of World War 1, World War 2 was a conflict with an obvious villain, Hitler, intent on seizing large swathes of Europe and exterminating anyone in his way. As such, fictional characters can be readily recognised as good and bad, and the story can reach a satisfying conclusion as good defeats evil.

Which other authors, fiction or non-fiction, do you admire who write about the Second World War?

Philip Kerr's Bernie Gunter series of novels offer tense and thrilling, but also illuminating pictures of life inside the Third Reich. It's interesting that after the war is over, Gunter's adventures seem less gripping.

Clive Ponting's biography, *Churchill,* pulls aside the curtain of myth which Churchill and his followers created, and which formed the dominant narrative until the 1980s. Churchill is revealed not as the man who saved Britain from Nazi rule, but as an aristocrat with attitudes and a worldview dating from the nineteenth century, whose actions were not always directed towards successful prosecution of the war, and who was rejected by most Britons at the polls once the war was over.

When the Doves Disappeared by Sofi Oksanen, set in Estonia in the early 1940s, when the country was ruled first by the Russians (since 1940) and then the Germans (1943-44), and then in the early 1960s when it was firmly in the Soviet grasp. The book shows how an unprincipled man repeatedly changes identity and uniform to fit into the prevailing regime, and carries out vicious acts on its behalf. The cynicism lying at the heart of authoritarian regimes is exposed.

If you could invite three figures from WW2 to dinner, who would they be and why?

Bernie Gunter, even though he's fictional, because he'd be good fun, and have lots of interesting anecdotes!

Inspector Foyle, another fiction character, created by Antony Horowitz, would be able to tell me exactly what things were like in Britain during the war years, and especially about the large amount of crime of all kinds that flourished in wartime.

By contrast, Dietrich Bonhoeffer was a pastor and theologian, who made the case during the Nazi period for Christians to stand up against the Nazi regime, and the moral emptiness it represented. He was hanged by the Nazis in April 1945, as the regime itself fell to pieces. Many fictional detectives, including my own Jüri Hallmets and Angus Blue, have a strong moral compass, and it would be good to discuss with Bonhoeffer the differences between law, justice, and morality.

What piece of advice would you give to other historical novelists out there, who are just starting out?

Do enough research to get your mind into the period and the place, so that your characters don't read like 21st-century people magicked into whatever period you're writing about. That will enable you to get their attitudes and motivations right.

Can you tell us a little more about your next project?

The third in the Estonia trilogy featuring Chief Inspector Jüri Hallmets. It's going to be called *The End of All Things*. That's because, in 1940, it was the end for independent Estonia, and Estonians would not be in command of their own destiny until they regained independence in 1991. So even though Jüri Hallmets may live to fight another day, the ending can't be for him a happy one. The Russians who seized the country from the Estonians in 1940, and again, this time from the Germans, in 1944, wiped out (literally) the intelligentsia and government officials, including middle-ranking and senior police officers. Hundreds of thousands of other ordinary citizens were sent to Siberia, to forced labour and concentration camps.

The Secret Listener by Deborah Swift

Seventeen-year-old Jim interlaced his fingers around Shirley's and wondered whether he dared to lean over and kiss her. The back row of the stalls was cramped and stank of cigarettes, and even getting her there had filled him with excruciating embarrassment. There was another couple there who had glared at them as they edged into the row in semi-darkness, grumbling as they were forced to move further along.

Now in the fusty dark of the cinema, the light from the projector streaming over his head through the smoke, he leant over and wrapped a hand around the back of Shirley's head. She turned and after a moment's awkward search in the dark, they were kissing.

The kissing went on until the end of the feature, when he realised he had only the sketchiest idea of what had happened in the film. Rather groggily, they stood up for the National Anthem before heading out into the cold air.

Jim clasped Shirley's hand tight. 'You'll be my girl, won't you?'

'I'm already your girl,' Shirley said, smiling.

'I mean, we can go steady?'

'Didn't feel very steady to me, Jim,' she said. 'In fact, I'd say we were going quite fast!'

The next day was a Thursday, and Shirley was studying, so he'd arranged to see her later. Wednesdays and Saturdays were their usual days because Shirley was only fifteen and still doing her Higher School Certificate, whereas he was working already as an apprentice at the Marconi radio factory. But today there was a dance on at the Palais, and Jim had said he'd take her.

Jim got changed into his best going-out suit, then settled down to listen to the wireless in front of the fire, which was smoking again because coal was rationed and they could only get coke.

'Can't get the blasted thing going,' his mother said, kneeling before the fire and holding a newspaper over the fireplace to encourage the draw. 'The kindling must be damp, and the coke won't take, blast it.'

His father didn't respond, deep as he was behind the London Standard, with a Capstan dangling from his lips, dangerously close to the newspaper. Jim's father worked for the London Dockyard – a reserved occupation – and they knew better than to disturb him for the first half an hour after work.

'He needs to let the steam out of his ears,' his mother always said, though quite what that meant, Jim had no idea.

When it got to six-thirty, Dad tuned the wireless in to get the Light Service and they settled down to enjoy 'It's That Man Again'. It had only just begun when there was a sharp rap at the front door.

As usual, his mother went to answer it. 'Collecting scrap metal again, I shouldn't wonder,' Dad called after her. 'Bloody cheek, this time of night.'

But a few moments later his mother reappeared in the back room, with a man in tow.

'Someone for you, Jim.' Her face already looked worried. 'Mr Smith.'

Jim stood up, surprised. The man was dressed in a neat grey mackintosh and bowler hat and had the bristling air of some kind of official. He even had a smart leather briefcase with a monogram on it. Oh gawd, what had he done now?

'Mr Bedford. Is there somewhere private we can talk?' he asked over the voices on the wireless. 'Where we won't be interrupted?'

Mother, completely flabbergasted by the air of superiority and the bowler hat, let alone him calling her son 'Mr Bedford', said: 'through there.' (If she could have bobbed a curtsey and said Your Majesty, she would have.) She hurried to open up the parlour, a room they only ever used for guests. It wasn't worth lighting a fire in two rooms, was it? And it was always warmer in the dining room right next to the kitchen.

The man sat himself down on the edge of one of the stiff upholstered chairs, opened up the briefcase, took out a paper and glanced at it. 'Ah yes, it was Mr Howe that recommended you.'

Jim sat down with a thump. Mr Howe. His boss. 'What is it? What've I done?'

'Nothing. We just want you to do a little job for us. Mr Howe tells us you know a bit about radios. He says you're good at decoding Morse code. A whizz at it, he said.'

'It's only a bit of fun, sir,' he said. 'We send each other messages when we're at work – things like 'the tea urn's on', stuff like that.'

'Mr Howe's impressed. Says you're a bright spark and honest.'

Jim frowned, suspicious. He thought he was in trouble, but now this all sounded a bit too glowing. Was Mr Smith trying to butter him up?

'Thing is, we need radio hams like you. We want you to try to find other people transmitting, people who might be German.'

Now Jim's jaw dropped. 'You mean, like a spy?'

More banging at the door. Cripes, it was Shirley. He'd forgotten all about her! He glanced at the clock – it was seven already. Mr Smith had said they weren't to be interrupted. What would his mother say to her?

So the whole time the man was talking, outlining how he'd have to write stuff down and how it was all top secret, Jim shuffled at the edge of his chair, hearing with one ear his mother telling Shirley that he couldn't come out because he had a terrible cold.

'But we were going to the Palais,' Shirley protested from the hall.

'Mr Bedford?' Mr Smith tapped his pen on his paper.

'Yes, I'm listening,' Jim said, dragging his attention back to his visitor.

'Now don't get too carried away,' the man said, 'it will be long hours and pretty boring. You'll need sharp, ears and the ability to concentrate and record exactly what you hear.'

Jim was already taken with the idea of catching Nazis in the act. He imagined them sat in some dark basement, dressed in full Nazi regalia, tapping out Morse.

In the background he could hear his mother telling Shirley he'd be in touch when he'd recovered. 'You don't want to catch it,' she said.

Jim struggled to concentrate as he heard the door slam. His heart cramped at the thought that Shirley was going away without him being able to see her and explain.

'What do you think?' the man asked, 'Will you help?'

'But does Mr Howe know? What about my other job at Marconi?'

'This is only part-time. Evenings, five days a week. You'll still need to do your Home Guard practices on Tuesdays and Sundays, and go to work as usual.'

Mr Smith seems to know an awful lot about me, Jim thought.

'You'll be paid, and we'll need to set aside a room for it.' Mr Smith glanced around. 'The equipment should fit in here quite nicely.'

'Hang on. I'll need to ask my mother. I'm not sure she'll be too pleased with the idea of me taking over her parlour.'

'That's the most important thing. You can't tell anyone what you're doing, not even your parents.'

'What? But how can they not know what I'm doing if I'm right here in the parlour?'

'You're a bright lad, you'll think of something.'

'Please, Mr Smith, won't you tell them something? Otherwise, they'll think I've done something awful and that I'm going to be arrested.'

As he showed him out, Mr Smith – was that really his name? – stuck his head around the dining room door, and in sonorous tones announced, 'Your son is going to be doing something very important for the war effort, for his country. I beg of you, ask no questions, and leave him to do it. It requires the utmost secrecy. Remember: Careless Talk Costs Lives.'

Jim saw his mother's mouth open and shut like a goldfish, but she said nothing. Dad just stared as if the words made no earthly sense, before saying, 'Our Jim?' as if the idea totally impossible.

'His mother said he had a terrible cold,' complained Shirley to her mother, 'but there was something odd about it. Mrs Bedford definitely looked nervous, and she wouldn't even let me in.'

'That's not like Jim. He usually sends a message. D'you think it's something infectious?'

'I don't know. But when I was standing on the doorstep I could hear a man's voice from the parlour, and there was a swanky car, a Humber, parked outside.'

'Probably the doctor. Though it would be odd of Mrs Bedford to call him out for just a cold.'

'Mr Smith came to see me last night,' Jim said to Mr Howe the next day at work. 'Thanks for recommending me.'

Mr Howe just winked and put a finger to his lips.

A few days later a van arrived at their house in Tooting, with an AR 88 radio receiver, a large black piece of equipment that he was supposed to hide in the bureau in the parlour. He looked at it askance. When it wouldn't fit in the top compartment of the bureau, they came back a few days later with a new bureau with a key, and to Mother's disgust, took their old one off to storage.

Jim stood over the most recent delivery, perplexed. There was an awful lot of stuff. Boxes of stationery, tons of it, and cartons of brand new pencils. When he opened the boxes, there were pads marked out in grids and with spaces to fill in the dates and the messages, and envelopes marked Top Secret. But at the sight of these he felt a frisson of excitement. Now he really did begin to fancy himself as a spy.

On Saturday he had to face Shirley.

'You feeling better?' she asked as they walked toward the high street.

'Yes, Just a cold.'

'You could have let me know.'

'It came on suddenly,' he said, wishing he'd thought to bring a handkerchief.

'And you're better now?'

'It was a flash in the pan thing,' he said, feeling his face grow hot and red under his freckles.

Shirley looked at him through narrowed eyes, and the rest of the night in the Copacabana coffee house, she wouldn't let him hold her hand.

Once he'd walked her home, he knew he had to broach it. 'The thing is,' he said, 'I won't be able to see you on Wednesdays any more. Only on Saturdays.' He rushed on before she could interrupt. 'There's this thing going on at work, and I've got to work late. It's an express order for the war effort.'

He saw her face crumple.

'It's not that I don't want to see you, it's just that I have to do this. Mr Howe insisted, and you don't want me to lose my job, do you?'

'Of course I don't. But it seems a bit rich, him ordering you about on your time off. And you do enough, what with the overtime you do already and your Home Guard duties.'

'But we all have to do extra because of the war.'

'War, war, war.' A heavy sigh. 'That's all I ever hear about these days. What hours do you have to do?'

He floundered. 'It's every night, until about nine o'clock.' He picked a figure out of the air. 'Sorry. It'll go back to normal once this rush is over.' He mentally crossed his fingers.

Shirley ran to catch up with her friend Betty as she was walking home from school. 'Can I come to yours on Wednesday?' Shirley asked. 'We can do our science homework together.'

''Course. But I thought Wednesday was the day you went out with Jim.'

'He can't do Wednesdays now – he's doing overtime.'

So the next Wednesday, she got the bus to Betty's and they spent the evening doing each other's hair and poring over their textbooks until Shirley had a bright idea. 'Hey, let's go and wait for Jim outside the factory. He finishes at nine.' She looked at her watch. 'It's a quarter past eight now, so not long to wait.'

They walked the fifteen minutes to the factory and in through the gates.

The long brick building was deserted. Not a sign of life. There were paper blackout blinds of course at the windows, but there were no cars or any sign of Jim's bicycle in the car park, and the doors were locked. The elderly security guard patrolling the site came around the corner.

'Is the factory shut?' Shirley asked.

'Aye. They finish at six o'clock. Why? Did you want something?'

'No, nothing,' Shirley said, grabbing Betty by the arm and dragging her away.

'Was anyone doing overtime today?' piped up Betty.

'No. They've all got night duties, like ARP warden. And because of night raids and bombing, no one works here after six.'

'I must have got it wrong,' Shirley said, trying to save face.

'He's lying to you,' Betty said. 'What a toad. You need to have it out with him.'

Meanwhile, at Jim's house, another chap, Mr Kent, younger and with a look of Cary Grant, was showing Jim what to do with the equipment. He'd telephoned earlier to say he was coming, and now was explaining the intricacies of the task.

'You will scan certain frequencies to detect any that might be from the *Abwehr*, the German Secret Service.'

'Which frequencies?' asked Jim.

Mr Kent handed Jim a sheet. 'Here's the list. Each secret listener has a different frequency. Look out for individual senders and try to recognise their sending style. Believe it or not, they often give themselves away with foolish banter. Some of these messages are even prefaced with HH.'

'HH?'

Mr Kent grinned. 'Heil Hitler.'

How stupid could Germans be? He wished he hadn't asked. What if his mother had heard Mr Kent? She might think he was working for the Germans.

When the training was done, he was asked to sign the Official Secrets Act prior to being enrolled as something called a volunteer interceptor, or VI.

It was both thrilling and frightening. But the lure of the equipment allayed any doubts. The whole shebang was up-to-the-minute and now he couldn't wait to get started, and to catch some of the enemy.

Before long he was happily tuning in through his headphones, oblivious to the outside world. He'd been a 'radio ham' for years. He and his friends were members of the radio club, and all their messages were in Morse. Jim was fluent in it. He loved listening through the blur of white noise to other amateur radio fans' greetings and chats, but when war broke out the government had suspended all amateur radio licences, so he was no longer able to send greetings or messages to his radio friends.

Jim concentrated on the static and crackle from the headphones, deep in the world he knew and understood.

There were several more training sessions whilst Jim got up to speed. His mother by now had got used to supplying the 'men from the ministry' with tea and whatever homemade biscuits she could eke from their rations. The men were insistent that nobody should see anything he was working on, and it all had to be locked away in the bureau after his 'listening' session.

On the following Wednesday, Jim was plugged in as usual, determined to find an enemy spy on English soil. Hunched over his receiver, headphones glued to his ears, he searched the airwaves for any signals that were not on official channels. His shoulders were stiff as wood and his pen hand cramped from writing things down at top speed. He was keenly aware of the responsibility – men's lives were at stake. He took pride in being diligent, even pernickety in his aim for total accuracy.

Outside Jim's house Shirley and Betty were negotiating the blackout to see if Jim was at home.

'How will we be able to tell?' Betty asked.

'His bicycle. He always chains it to the drain pipe.'

They crept along arm in arm until they came to Jim's house, a tall brick-built terrace.

'Will you look at that!' Shirley said, spotting the bicycle. 'He's actually in there.'

'Well, why won't he come out and see you? Betty said. 'It's weird. There's something fishy going on.'

'Let's go around the back, see if we can see anything.'

The two girls crept down the narrow alley next to the house and into the back yard. 'Ooh its spooky round here,' Betty whispered, as they navigated past the dustbins and coal bunker. The parlour window was blacked out, but they still couldn't see anything. 'You'll have to knock,' Betty insisted. 'See if he'll come out.'

Shirley braced herself and knocked. Mrs Bedford came to the door. 'Oh. Shirley.' She didn't look pleased to see her.

'Is Jim in?'

'He's busy. He's... he's in the bath.'

'He told me he was working late, doing overtime.'

'Ah well, he was...earlier. But now he's in the bath.'

'Then I'll wait for him.'

'No, it's too late to be courting tonight. You go on home. I'll get him to call round to your house about the weekend.' With that, she closed the door.

Betty's eyebrows shot up. 'Well! How rude was that?'

'Maybe he is in the bath,' Shirley said doubtfully.

'Not a chance. She's lying. The absolute bounder! I bet he's seeing someone else,' Betty said, 'and keeping you dangling like a fool. I'd dump him if I were you.'

Shirley didn't reply. She was too hurt.

Jim tuned into the shortwave radio bands as instructed, and told no one. Smith, the man from the ministry, had put the fear of God into him, telling him that dire punishment awaited anyone who blabbed. After a while, clues in the transmissions, like blocks of five letters, made him suspect he was tuning into German *Abwehr* frequencies, though he could never be certain, and had been told not to try to do anything about any suspicion but merely record it letter for letter.

Though dying to know if the men he was listening to were really German spies, he simply did his job, then posted the results off to the mysterious PO Box 25, Barnet.

It was tantalising though, to think he was tuning in to enemy agents, right here in the suburbs of South London. He worried though about Shirley. She'd been off-hand with him on Saturday, and he knew it was because it was odd that he could no longer see her in the week, when their Wednesdays used to be so regular.

'What about another night?' she'd insisted. 'I know you can't do Wednesdays, but what about Thursdays?'

'I told you, I can't do any night,' he said. 'I know I said it was overtime, but I'm working from home.'

'Well, that's alright then. No reason why I can't come around and keep you company.'

'No! You can't do that.'

'Why not?'

'It's just, I need to concentrate, and it's very fiddly work.'

'You're making excuses. What is it with you, Jim? Are you seeing someone else?'

'Of course I'm not. Just bear with it for a few more weeks, then we'll be back to how we were. It's the work. I can't explain.'

'Well, call me when you *are* ready to explain.' She turned away and marched off down the street.'

He ran to catch up with her. 'Aww Shirley. I care about you, honest. Just give me a few more weeks.'

'He's got another girlfriend,' Betty said, 'Bet you.'

'No, I think it's something else.'

'What else could it be? I think you should go round there on Wednesday, see if you can catch them at it.'

'I don't think –'

'It would sort it out once and for all.'

So, at Betty's prompting, the following Wednesday Shirley hammered at the Bedfords' door.

Mrs Bedford opened it as usual, but before she could say a word, Shirley and Betty pushed past her into the house and into the dining room.

'Where is he?' Betty said.

'Now just you wait a minute,' Mr Bedford said, standing up from his chair.

But Betty was already throwing open the door to the parlour, with Shirley right behind her.

What they saw was Jim's hunched back, and a lot of black equipment with trailing wires. 'What the heck is all this?' Shirley said.

Jim turned and his face drained of colour. He ripped off his headphones.

'What are you doing, Jim?' Shirley took in the barrage of radio equipment.

'He's spying for the Germans,' Betty said. 'That's what he's doing. That's why it's so hush hush. That's why he couldn't tell you. Come on, we're going for the police.'

'Shirley! Stop! Let me explain!'

She folded her arms. 'Go on then. I'm waiting.'

'I...I just –' Jim gulped back the words. He knew he could say nothing. He'd signed the official secrets act, hadn't he?

The two girls rushed out, leaving Jim white-faced in the parlour.

Jim charged after them, straight past his concerned parents in the hall. He looked frantically up and down the street, to see the girls just heading around the corner towards the underground station. He sprinted to catch them, blood pounding in his ears. He'd never run so fast in his life.

'Shirley! Wait!' he yelled.

She turned, but her face was wet with angry tears. 'Don't you dare come near me! You traitor.'

'I'm not a traitor. It's for our side. Please just let me talk for a moment.'

'Don't listen to him,' Betty said.

'And you keep your nose out of it,' Jim said. 'It's none of your business. This is between me and Shirley.'

Betty opened her mouth, but Shirley cut her off. 'It's all right Betty, I'll give him two minutes.'

'Well, don't say I didn't warn you next time he tells you a load of old porkies.' Betty flounced off and into the underground station.

'I'm sorry Shirley,' Jim said. 'I really can't tell you anything about what I'm doing. But you can ask Mother and she'll tell you it really is for our government. I'd never do anything to deliberately hurt you.'

'Then why didn't you just say? Or tell me?'

'It's top secret. I had to swear I wouldn't.' He reached out to embrace her. She let him enfold her in a hug. 'And now I have to make sure you won't tell either. We can be in it together.'

'In what though?'

He released her so he could look into her eyes. 'It has to be secret. Not even Betty can know.'

'But she saw all that stuff.'

'Then you'll have to tell her I'm testing equipment for Marconi – some new kind of radio system. Can you do that?'

She was still tearful. 'How do I know I can trust you?'

'Because I'm just Jim, from the factory down the road. Jim, who thinks the world of you.' He touched a finger to her cheek.

Shirley crumpled against his chest. 'I was just afraid you'd got someone else.'

'You silly thing. There's never been anyone else. Except my job to help win this ghastly war. And when it's over, I promise you, we'll make up for all that lost time.'

She lifted her chin, and he kissed her long and deep, until the pain in his chest dissolved, and he felt his heart might want to lift up and fly away.

'Swear you're working for us and not the Germans.'

He stood back away from her. 'Do I look like a Nazi? Have I ever owned a pair of jack boots?' She giggled and looked down at his knitted socks and well-worn lace-ups. 'Shirley love, I swear,' he said. 'It's government war work. And while I'm at it, I swear you are the only one for me, and one day soon I'll take you down the aisle at All Saints and prove it.'

Author's note. This is a story based loosely on the true story of Ray and Barbara Faultley, and it did have a happy ending – Ray and Barbara did eventually get married. Because of the Official Secrets Act, Ray kept the secret about what he was doing in his front parlour for many years of their marriage.

There were about 1,500 other Voluntary Interceptors, amateur radio buffs who analysed the Morse from thousands of messages and relayed this sensitive and vital information via listening stations to those at Bletchley Park and beyond. More about The Secret Listeners can be found here in the National Archive.

Interview

Can you first please tell us a little more about the series and/or character that your short story is based around?

I am currently writing a series of books all of which feature radio communication in WW2. The first one, *The Silk Code*, about the Baker Street decoders, will be out in May 2023. It features the women who were tasked with decoding 'indecipherables' – messages from agents in the field that had been scrambled or become impossible to decode. What will they do when they discover the agents they are decoding have been infiltrated by the enemy? The second novel, coming soon after that, is about the creation of radio, and the 'black' propaganda or 'fake news' relayed to Germany. And there will be a third about a radio operator in Nazi-occupied Holland.

What first attracted you to the period you write about? How do you approach researching your novels?

World War Two is full of stories of courage, and also of unsung heroes. Who doesn't love a hero?! I've enjoyed researching little-known heroes of the era, but I also love to fictionalise the story so I can draw out parallels with the contemporary concerns of the day. My research consists of reading many non-fiction books and eyewitness accounts, and also trawling through academic websites for specialist information. One thing I have found particularly useful is old newspapers and magazines of the era, which give 'on the ground' information not only about politics and the machinations of war, but also of domestic concerns, the sort of products you were able to buy, reports from the courts, and the attitude of the general public.

If there was one moment in history you could witness, featured in one of your novels, what would it be?

I love reunions. I'm a sucker for watching people who love each other come together after years apart. Wartime railway stations fascinate me! I would have loved to have been a fly on the wall when Peter comes home to his mother after five years in a German Prisoner of War camp (from my book *Past Encounters*). And of course, these reunions are never what one might expect!

What do you think makes so many readers attracted to reading about the Second World War?
Possibly because we are glad we don't have to face it ourselves. At the same time, we can imagine what it was like for ordinary people to have to live through those extraordinary times. It makes us more readily able to empathise with those in war-torn countries, wherever they are.

Which other authors, fiction or non-fiction, do you admire who write about the Second World War?
I have particularly enjoyed *Bodyguard of Lies* by Anthony Cave Brown. This is a huge book, about deceptions carried out in WW2. It is now very dated – published in 1976, but for a novelist, it is a superb insight and chock-full of interest and anecdotes.

If you could invite three figures from WW2 to dinner, who would they be and why?
No-one! I worry I might hate them for certain views that have moved on in society since then, and they were a product of their time, not ours. I'd happily spend a lonely night watching old black-and-white WW2 movies instead.

What piece of advice would you give to other historical novelists out there, who are just starting out?
There will be lots of conflicting advice! Accept it all, and sift out what speaks to you and keep that. After all, every writer's book is unique, and the vision for your book can't be solved by any sort of formula. There is no 'one way' to write a book or make it a success, so enjoy the process of writing and researching, rather than obsessing about what will happen once it's written.

Can you tell us a little more about your next project?

I'm in the middle of writing a series of books about Secret Agents so the third book in the series is engaging me, and I'm researching the Hunger Winter in Holland. I'm wrestling with that right now, and it makes me extremely grateful to be warm and fed! The first in the series of books is *The Silk Code*, out May 2023.

PQ18, by Matthew Willis

The Woolworth carrier *Avenger* had barely clawed out of Seyðisfjörður with a Hunt-class on each beam when the engines stopped.

In the wardroom, Lieutenant Edmund Clydesdale and the others from 802 Squadron sat up like gundogs. Silence, and the unruly slop of waves. They rushed on deck as if the reason for the stoppage would somehow be more apparent in the open air. Someone nipped to the compass platform to find out, and returned like Pheidippides from Marathon.

"The engines have stopped," he intoned, to a barrage of catcalls.

It was a grand evening, and there was a lot of it considering there'd only be two hours of darkness. Edmund inhaled a lungful of sharp Iceland air and admired the tumbled outline of the island against the ruddy dusk. The destroyers were holding station, nervously darting back and forth as if shifting from foot to foot. Edmund remembered U-boats with a roiling in his midriff. Just a few weeks ago he'd been strapped into his Hurricane waiting for the launch, heard a series of reports and looked up to see HMS *Eagle* in the next column slowly rolling over. Three torpedoes had got her, right in the middle of the convoy. That was in the Med, all sparkling waves and glaring sun and now he was on his way to the Arctic. It was like another world. Another life.

He stayed on deck, shuffling and blowing streamers of white mist, while most slunk back to the wardroom, and only followed when his hands lanced with pain even trapped under his arms.

Three hours the engines remained silent. One by one, the pilots left to turn in. Special Duty officers' cabins were down below the hangar, right where a torpedo would bury itself an instant before ripping the ship to burning shreds. Sometime after midnight it was only Edmund trying not to drum his fingers on the table, and Lucas, browsing Picture Post, and the steward, flitting impatiently. Edmund was clenching his teeth again. When did that headache come on?

Just when he was certain they'd have to tow the carrier back into port, with a clank and a rumble deep below, the engines started.

Lucas glanced up from the page he'd been staring at for the last hour. "Oh, are we going again?"

The rumbling changed tone and the idle slopping became a regular heave. "I'd say we are now, thank goodness," Edmund replied.

"Hullo, what's this?"

Edmund looked up. A figure, hatless, in overalls, oil-smeared, had entered the wardroom. It shambled in the direction of the galley hatch. In the wardroom! Edmund felt the tension in his muscles coalesce into a surge of hot rage. "Hey, what the blazes do you think you're doing in here?"

The figure stopped after a moment. A face, zebra-striped with grime and sweat turned towards them. Lurid eyes stared, unseeing.

"I said what are you doing in here?" Edmund cleared his throat. His voice was catching. "This is the wardroom."

The figure stared for a moment longer and then something seemed to click into place and he straightened. "I'm an officer. This is where I mess."

"Well 'mess' is the word," Lucas muttered.

"But..." Edmund limply gestured at the man's overalls. He opened and closed his mouth. It had gone dry.

"Just came in here for a cup of tea," the figure said. "Only got ten minutes and then back to the bloody engines again. Well you can keep your sodding wardroom!"

The door slammed and the figure was gone.

"They let all sorts in now," Lucas murmured.

"An officer?" Edmund massaged his temple. The engines seemed to be throbbing at the precise frequency of his headache. "Oh! One of the Subbie E lot?"

Lucas was back in his Picture Post. "Exactly. Not a real officer at all. Don't know why they commissioned them. Their Lordships move in mysterious ways." He huffed and rearranged his magazine. "He may mess here, but not dressed like that!"

Now it made sense. *Avenger* had a dozen 'Sub-Lieutenant E RNR' on the books, reservists plucked from the Merchant Navy and dumped in the Woolworth carriers as junior engineers. As if to remind the Navy personnel they were not serving on a warship at all, but a merchantman with a flight deck slapped onto the hull. Lucas looked at the door and pulled a face.

Edmund was a grammar school boy, and it never took long in the Fleet Air Arm to be reminded of it. "I'm just glad they got the engines going again," he sighed. "Wasn't keen on being a sitting duck for U-boats any longer."

"It's the *Tirpitz* I'm worried about."

"At least we'll see the *Tirpitz* coming."

"I wouldn't bet on it, the weather we get up here."

Edmund felt suddenly awkward. Foolish and cheap for snapping at the engineer, cowardly for the fear that still wound his insides even with the ship moving again. He turned in, dog-tired but awake, left leg full of twitch and the right one threatening to join in. Every noise jolted him further awake. Oh god, if only he could just climb into a Hurricane and fly, he'd know what to do.

The morning dawned grey and violent, slabs of charcoal sea concussing the carrier. There'd been a blizzard in the night. The ship glittered like a comet. Splinters of frozen snow nestled in nooks where they'd gathered. It was only mid-September. Rain showers, brief and brutal, dulled the air and glittered the decks.

They brought half a dozen aircraft up from the hangar and tried to range a patrol. Edmund watched the deck party wrestle airframes against the wind, pelted by spray. It was getting worse, wasn't it? A flurry of gusts, a bigger-still wave, and he saw the maintainers, shouts silenced by the wind, shock stamped on white faces as a Sea Hurricane wrenched out of their grip and skated a dozen yards across the deck. On the backroll they almost caught it, and then the carrier pitched again and the Hurricane was sliding, lurching into the catwalk, one wing in the air, then hanging like a detonated chimney, over, over and gone. The deck party solemnly lashed the remaining aircraft in place, covered the engines with tarps, and trudged below. One aircraft lost and they hadn't even got off the deck yet!

It was too much up on the flight deck. The violence of wind and cold. It was too close down below, the passageways and flats pressing in on him. He found his way to the quarterdeck, nestling below the after end of the flight deck. Clean, Arctic air, fresh as issued by the storesman that morning. The Oerlikon was covered and unmanned – too rough for enemy aircraft – and there was only one other person there, hunched over the rail, collar turned up. They turned, and Edmund started. Balls! He wouldn't have recognised the face, not with all that muck on it the other day, but those eyes, blue as thunder. For a moment he was ready to turn tail. But it still weighed on him. He took a step forward.

"Look, I'm sorry about last night. In the wardroom. It was rude."

"Oh. That." The other looked astern again, then turned back. "It's alright. I can't get used to all this Navy faff."

"It does seem silly sometimes. The rules, I mean. But I shouldn't have barked at you." Edmund adjusted his scarf, blew on his hands. "Truth is, I was a bit spooked. By the engines being out."

The engineer nodded. "I dare say. Didn't have time to be, meself. Needed all the engine room crew on it. Bloody American junk. I wish they'd give us a proper steam powerplant. This diesel..." There was a burr to his accent. Liverpool?

"What was the problem?"

The other snorted. "What wasn't? Sand and water sludge in the fuel. We had the engine in bits trying to clean it all out."

Edmund felt another crunch of guilt. While he'd been sitting in comfort sipping gin, the engineers had been up to their elbows in muck and scrap. Furiously trying to get the old tub moving. Now they were flat-out trying to catch the convoy and likely taking all the crew's efforts to keep the engines working.

"Christ." He sighed. "You must've been cream-crackered and I threw you out on your ear."

"It wasn't just you. I was alright. Got tea in the NAAFI."

"Well, nevertheless. You've as much right as anyone, as far as I'm concerned."

The engineer laughed. "Honestly, I wish they'd just call us ERAs and give us a mess on the lower deck. We'd prefer it. I dare say you lot would too."

"Oh I don't know. I think the Navy could do with a bit of shaking up. Look, my name's Clydesdale. People call me Clyde." He offered his hand.

The other took it. "Fletcher. You a pilot?"

"Yes, Hurricanes."

Fletcher smiled. "Great stuff. Good little engine. Make sure you keep the bombers off our back will you?"

"I'll do my best," Edmund gulped.

"Well, ta-ta. I'd better get back to that sack of bolts down below."

Edmund felt instantly lighter, a sensation that was soon replaced by a churning in his gut. He rushed to the thunderbox, shuddered reflexively at the cold of seat on skin, and sat for five minutes staring at the back of the door.

A little later the wind and sea moderated enough for flying. A Swordfish staggered off the deck and began a lazy orbit, scanning for submarines. By the end of the day they'd caught up with convoy PQ18, and *Avenger* slotted in aft of the second column. Edmund gazed admiringly at the rows of stubby tramps and prostrate tankers. What a wizard target they'd make for a U-boat.

Later still, a dysphony of alarms shrieked through the ship. *Special dutymen to your stations.* Edmund crawled into his flying kit. *Green and Pink Flights to readiness.* That was him. The maintainers brought up another Hurricane from the hangar, so there were four perching on the afterdeck. The carrier was describing the motion of a corkscrew.

Check controls, trim, everything ready to start the engine. Gunsight? Brightness minimum. Wingspan seventy feet, nicely between a Junkers and a Heinkel. Damn this cold! Dart of pain in the fingerjoints-cold, even with two pairs of gloves. Lungs scoured-out with every breath-cold. Feet disappearing into numb oblivion-cold. *Fighters at readiness, launch!* He primed the engine, hit the starter, the Merlin whine-cough-crashed into a lumpy growl and the mechanics disconnected the trolley-acc. Sharkey Ward in the lead Hurri opened his throttle and the fighter trundled sluggishly down the deck, vanished off the end as the carrier pitched upwards. It was an aeon before the bow came down

91

again...and there was Ward's Hurricane, limping at wavetop height, scratching for altitude. Phew.

Finally, Edmund could open the throttle, and felt the Hurricane strain against the brakes. Let the tail come up in the slipstream, balancing on the mainwheels, the view opening up over the bow to the churning sea. Then let the brakes off and feel the aircraft lunge, and airborne.

The R/T was crackling and fizzing, the fighter director talking to Sharkey. The four Hurricanes formed up. There was a big Focke-Wulf Kurier snooping. The cloud was barely at five hundred feet, and there were patches of mist hanging on the surface.

It was supposed to be dead ahead. Less than a mile. But there was nothing. Just grey sky, wisps of darker torn-rag billowing across. And then. Something, seen as an irritation in his vision. A too-regular shape skimming the wavetops. "There it is, Green Leader. Ten o'clock, low." A slender, four-engined thing, all elegant lines but bristling with guns.

"I see him."

Edmund checked his guns were armed. Ward banked, his wingtip almost carving a furrow in the sea, and Edmund fought to stay on station. There! Jerry kite, the same colour as the sea. Almost lined up, his thumb hovering over the button. A black cross momentarily silhouetted against the white. Tracers darted at him, floating like embers. He got off a burst but the next moment the Kurier had simply vanished.

"Where the hell is he?"

"Gone into cloud. Hello *Avenger*, I need a fix on that bandit."

They groped about, catching the odd glimpse, but the Jerry was canny and using the cover skilfully. After half an hour their fuel was low. Edmund caught a glimpse, at about two miles, the Kurier trundling serenely on its way. Bastard.

They landed, chafing with frustration and, once debriefed, Edmund stomped to the quarterdeck. As if expecting him, Fletcher was there again, a bit apart from a gaggle of junior officers.

"Oh hallo." He smiled and offered Edmund a Players. "Did you get anything?"

Edmund grimaced. "Not a sausage. Jerry was too clever for us. Look, d'you fancy coming to the wardroom for a bit? I'll buy you a cup of tea."

"Ah." Fletcher shook his head "Thanks. Haven't got time really. Need to get back soon. Your lot are going to be flying all day, engines'll be at full stretch. And besides..." He indicated his overalls.

Edmund flushed and could find nothing to say. Fletcher lit himself another cigarette and sportingly, gestured at the ranks of merchant ships plugging through the swell. "What d'you reckon they've got us carting all this stuff to Russia for? Not like we couldn't use it ourselves. All that petrol. Tanks. Ammo."

"You're telling me," Edmund sighed. "Can't afford to let Hitler take Russia I s'pose. They've tons of oil, ore and whatnot. Factories. Can't have the Nazis getting hold of it all and turning it on us."

"Hmph." Fletcher hunched his shoulders. "Hope they make good use of it."

"They told us it'll just be for a while. 'Til the Jerries get in too deep."

"Maybe. Ah well." Fletcher smiled brightly and looked away from the staggering merchantmen. You got any family?"

"Parents in Devon. And, uh, well. Girl in Malta." Girl! He grinned at the thought of how Liena would react to being described that way.

Fletcher's eyes widened. "Malta? Blimey. How'd you swing that?"

"I was in the Med until a couple of weeks ago. *Indomitable*. CO copped a packet, squadron disbanded, aircrew dispersed. And, here I am." His grin faded, and he shrugged. "Don't know if I'll ever see her again. Or if she'll want anything to do with me if I do. How about you?"

"Family in Birkenhead. Seeing a girl in Glasgow when I can get leave. Usual story. Malta, eh? I'd love to see it."

And then the tannoy was crackling, *All fighters to readiness*, and they muttered good-lucks and farewells, and Edmund promised to buy Fletcher a drink later and he could ask about Malta all he liked.

A hurried squadron briefing – big raids expected soon, the morning's efforts had persuaded the CO to put up a constant patrol into the air. They'd be flat out into the evening. So would the ship.

Eighty plus bandits inbound.

The standing patrol was vectored on, the pair at readiness launched. Frantically, the squadron maintainers brought the remaining Hurricanes up from the hangar, launching them as they were ready. Edmund waited his turn. A ripple of concussion drifted over the water. The destroyers were putting up a barrage, a carpet of woolly black puffs whooshing into sudden life above the merchantmen. Torpid Oerlikon tracers spurted skyward, yellow, turning red as they climbed against the gloom. "Don't they look gay?" someone said.

Now he could see the bombers through gaps in the cloud, black stitches on grey fabric. A forest of spouts erupted from the water, then another, a tower of smoke and flame gushed skywards, enveloping the sea where a ship had been. The nauseous bloom tumbled, and as *Avenger* passed, a sprinkling of dust pattered on the deck. Not dust. Ash. The column was well astern when the smoke cleared enough to see all that remained, an oily smear and fragments lolling on the surface. Jesus. Edmund stomach lurched and he swallowed bitter vomit. Don't throw up in the cockpit, for goodness' sake.

Finally, it was Edmund's turn to launch. His Hurricane raced off the deck and there were *forty-plus bandits approaching zero-eight-zero, nought feet, Green Section to intercept*. There they were, spaced out in a row, like something from another planet, twin-engine jobs distended with torpedoes.

He shoved the throttle wide, hung on, and picked a Heinkel right in the middle. It was coming on fast, just a little lead, drifting to the left. He let his thumb fall softly onto the button, felt the thunk as it triggered, the muffled hammering of eight Brownings, ribbon streams of tracer flicked out, scattering the bomber in flashes. It was still coming on, ludicrously fast, and he heaved the stick back, feeling the Hurricane buck, somewhere in his brain he registered the Heinkel turning aside. It hardly felt like anything at all, but the formation was bursting like a flock of starlings when a car backfired. A sudden feeling of immense power, as if he'd kicked a house and watched it crumble. But there was no time. He picked another Heinkel and dived at it.

It felt like mere moments but his ammo was gone, his fuel nearly, and he thumped the Hurricane back onto the carrier just as another wave of them came in. The sky was white and dirty brown with waterspouts, a grotesque hail of spray and debris rattling on the wings and the ship was upending, sliding into the black but no, it was just vertigo, they were safe. Safe! Edmund uttered a sob, and then there was more work to do. Swarming bombers plastering the ships with high explosive. Torpedo bombers darting at them like terriers. The Hurricanes did what they could. It was evening when Edmund swung his fighter into the landing pattern for the last time that day, the skies finally clear. On the downwind leg he caught a glimpse of *Avenger*'s flanks, scarred with bursts from near-misses, the plates of the hull punctured like paper.

Fletcher wasn't on the quarterdeck, just a damage control party heaving sacks over the side.

He tried the wardroom, then the junior officers' berths, then the unfamiliar levels of the engine room. In a flat that stank of creosote he collared an engineer.

"Fletch? Bought it. That last attack. Caught shrapnel in the neck."

It couldn't be, and yet Edmund had known it. "Oh. Oh god. Do you think? Ah, did he? Was it?"

"Doubt he knew what hit him."

He could not be alone. Edmund sloped to the wardroom. There was a regular party in progress. He helped himself to gin and slumped by the other pilots.

Lucas hailed him. "What a circus! Get anything? I was just telling Minty about that grease-monkey who wandered in here last night. Luckily he hasn't put in a reappearance. Good job you saw him off or we'd need to have a word with the Warrant Gunner."

Edmund stared, not letting himself move or twitch or think. "If it weren't for that grease-monkey," he muttered softly, "you'd never have got off the deck." He stood, quivering.

Lucas peered over the top of his drink. "Alright, no need to be like that. Where are you off to?"

"Never you mind." Edmund scanned the wardroom for the Subbie Es. A few were gathered on a table in the far corner, and he struck out towards them against the roll of the ship.

Interview

Can you first please tell us a little more about the series and/or character that your short story is based around?

PQ18 follows the *Fortress of Malta* series, which is about a Fleet Air Arm fighter pilot, Edmund Clydesdale, during the height of the Battle of Malta when the Royal Navy made a last-ditch effort to force supply convoys through to the embattled island. Clydesdale is a bit of a loner and unsure of himself when we first meet him. It takes the cauldron of combat and the people he meets along the way for him to realise his worth and his place in the war.

What first attracted you to the period you write about? How do you approach researching your novels?

I've been interested in Second World War aviation for almost as long as I can remember. As a boy, I loved reading Commando and War Picture Library comics, and my favourites were Fleet Air Arm stories. As far as research is concerned, I'm lucky that I'm also a non-fiction writer. On several occasions, I've been conducting research for non-fiction and come across a source that makes me think 'this would make an amazing novel.' Then it's a case of finding what you need to make it authentic, whether that's very formal dispatches or personal accounts of people who were there and everything in between. I've been lucky enough to interview a number of WW2 veterans over the years and it's possible to get a feel for how people were back then, how they approached these seismic events.

If there was one moment in history you could witness, featured in one of your novels, what would it be?

The height of the air attacks on Operation Pedestal in the afternoon of 12 August 1942. I can hardly imagine what it was like with wave after wave of bombers coming in, the air filled with ack-ack and a dwindling assemblage of fighters trying like fury to keep them at bay – only for one of the carriers, *Indomitable*, to be set upon by Stukas just an hour before she was due to turn back for Gibraltar. That meant many of the pilots had to try to land on the one remaining carrier, *Victorious*. It was an afternoon that the course of the war in the Mediterranean turned on.

What do you think makes so many readers attracted to reading about the Second World War?

I suppose it's the combination of relative recency and the sheer scale and importance of the conflict. People my age, mid-40s, will have grown up with people of our grandparents' generation who lived through the war and will have heard stories about it from them, and just about everyone was involved in some way, whether it was at the front or in the Home Guard, ARP, Land Army and so on. Because that generation was still very much part of the furniture in the 1980s, the Second World War still felt like a living part of the national makeup. We also have the wave of revisionist assessments and re-evaluations of the old versions of the story, and I think that has created new interest in a number of areas.

Which other authors, fiction or non-fiction, do you admire who write about the Second World War?

There aren't many authors tackling this work that I don't admire, but in particular in non-fiction I have to mention Will Iredale who has such a great knack for presenting superbly researched history in a way that's as compelling as the best novels. Richard Overy's heavyweight reappraisal of the entire Second World War, 'Blood and Ruins', was not just an important book but an enjoyable one in its way. I found Overy's ability to weave a cohesive thesis from such a wide-ranging subject to be really impressive, and it chimes with the way I try to approach things.

If you could invite three figures from WW2 to dinner, who would they be and why?

I'd better be careful who I put at the same table! First would be Lydia Vladimirovna Litvyak, the female Soviet fighter ace, whose experiences and rebellious, ebullient character would be sure to make the occasion buzz. I've got to have someone from the Fleet

98

Air Arm so I'll choose Roy Baker-Falkner, leader of one of the Fairey Barracuda Squadrons in the Tirpitz attacks in 1944. And finally, George Steer, who started off as a war correspondent, reporting on war crimes in Guernica and Abyssinia, and then helped develop offensive uses of propaganda in Burma. He's the inspiration for Vickery, my recurring war correspondent character but I've no doubt in this case that the facts are much more compelling than fiction could be.

What piece of advice would you give to other historical novelists out there, who are just starting out?
Start with research. Read what interests you, plenty of it, and the stories and characters will emerge by themselves and be authentic. It's both harder and less effective to try to create stories and characters and then fit the history around them.

Can you tell us a little more about your next project?
I'm working on several things but the one closest to completion is a novel about an American fighter-bomber squadron in the Mediterranean theatre in 1943. I'm really looking forward to it seeing the light of day as I've been working on it off and on for around a decade!

Printed in Great Britain
by Amazon

43897210R00057